GOAGR@M

GOAGR@M

Misadventures of an influencer

BINA NAYAK

HarperCollins *Publishers* India

First published in India by HarperCollins *Publishers* 2024
4th Floor, Tower A, Building No. 10, DLF Cyber City,
DLF Phase II, Gurugram, Haryana – 122002
www.harpercollins.co.in

2 4 6 8 10 9 7 5 3 1

Copyright © Bina Nayak 2024

P-ISBN: 978-93-5699-571-0
E-ISBN: 978-93-5699-572-7

This is a work of fiction and all characters and incidents described in this book are the product of the author's imagination. Any resemblance to actual persons, living or dead, is entirely coincidental.

Bina Nayak asserts the moral right
to be identified as the author of this work.

All rights reserved. No part of this publication may be reproduced, stored in a retrieval system, or transmitted, in any form or by any means, electronic, mechanical, photocopying, recording or otherwise, without the prior permission of the publishers.

Typeset in 11/14.7 Adobe Garamond at
Manipal Technologies Limited, Manipal

Printed and bound at
Thomson Press (India) Ltd.

This book is produced from independently certified FSC® paper
to ensure responsible forest management.

Contents

PART I

Chapter 1	*Dear Zindagi* Road	3
Chapter 2	Kalkaji to Panaji	9
Chapter 3	Almost Famous	15
Chapter 4	#BestLife	23
Chapter 5	Tall Glass of Russian	35
Chapter 6	Everybody's Vloggin'	40
Chapter 7	Gone in Two Seconds	56
Chapter 8	Video Killed the Radio Star	63

PART II

Chapter 9	Between a Dank and a Dark Place	71
Chapter 10	Not Feni	78
Chapter 11	Fairy Godfather	84
Chapter 12	Demons at Mapusa Bus Stand	89
Chapter 13	Let Us Rest in Pieces	98

Chapter 14	To Everything Turn, Turn, Turn	104
Chapter 15	Funeral Blues	110
Chapter 16	All Is Not, Well, Water	119
Chapter 17	Ghosts of Weddings Past	128

PART III

Chapter 18	Fuchsia Fashion	137
Chapter 19	Finders Keepers	143
Chapter 20	Cop-out	146
Chapter 21	The Hack Job	153
Chapter 22	Fashionistas Conquistas	162
Chapter 23	Blog-Vlog	173
Chapter 24	Straightjacketed Angel	180
Chapter 25	*Bambai Sé Aaya Mera Dost*	186
Chapter 26	Runaway Girls	195
Chapter 27	Get Out! Into the Spotlight	206
Chapter 28	Banking on Success	213
Chapter 29	Yesterday, Once More	216
Chapter 30	Heyy! Mona …	226
Chapter 31	Shanky-Panky	237
Chapter 32	Fashionably Mad	249
	Acknowledgements	257

In memory of my mother's seamstress days

PART I

PART I

CHAPTER 1

Dear Zindagi Road

She rides in the trajectory of a falling object, lost in the chatter inside her head. The object smashes her scooter's headlight, bounces off its front fender and somersaults five times on the asphalt. Like a decapitated head. Madhur screeches to a halt, her heart pummelling inside her mouth. A Delhi Traffic Police billboard flashes in her mind's eye—*Kripaya Helmet Pehney.* (Please wear a helmet.) She thinks—who threw such a big rock?

But it can't be a rock; there is no one around and no tall buildings to launch projectiles from. She is on a narrow road, fenced on both sides by coconut palms, the heavily laden trees eager to lighten their burden on unsuspecting passers-by. She spots the 'rock'—it's actually a coconut—lying on the road. Madhur remembers a few viral videos of people being killed by falling coconuts. '*Ab kya?* Do I have to wear a helmet wherever I go? Even on a two-minute ride to the corner cigarette shop?' she mutters to herself.

Checking furtively if anyone's watching, she retrieves the errant coconut and stashes it inside her scooter's boot. The nut may have dented her scooter, but there's no way it's going to dent her confidence. Taking a deep breath, she composes herself and gets back on the scooter to continue with the rest of her day.

Madhur: Hello friends! I'm Madhur Chopra, and I'm on the famous *Dear Zindagi* road in Parra, Goa. It's a lovely Sunday today, as you can see.

She pans her mobile towards the horizon to show two parallel columns of coconut palms meeting down the narrow road. On both sides of the road, vast tracts of rice fields are stretched out. In the distance there are dark hills with little specks of white dwellings—a chapel here, a bungalow there.

MADHUR: *Kaun kahega ki India mein COVID chal raha hain?* (Who'll say there's COVID raging in India?) Here in Goa, there's nothing! *Doston, agar aap ghar mein quarantined hain, toh yé khubsoorat nazaara khaas aap ké liyé!* (Friends, if you're quarantined at home, this beautiful view is just for you!)

She switches her mobile camera to selfie mode.

MADHUR: Friends, as you can see, I'm not wearing a mask. I'm in Goaaa! I'm safe here, *lekin aap please mask péhné* (but you, please wear a mask). This is Madhur Chopra, aapki favourite Instagrammer, signing out. We'll meet again tomorrow. *Tab tak aap mujhey* comments

> *mein bataa di jiyé ki* (Till then, let me know in the comments) what you all want to see in Goa. So doston, stay safe and goodbye from Goaaaaa!

She uploads the video to her social media accounts, checks her feed and puts her mobile away.

Madhur walks to her scooter and turns the ignition key. But the engine does not respond. Could the coconut have caused this? She tries the kick start. After ten minutes of kicking, she starts to sweat profusely; her sheer white mini dress gets completely soaked and sticks to her body, making her feel icky. It is 9.00 a.m. and the sun has gone from soothing to roasting strength in a space of fifteen minutes. But it's not Goa's heat that bothers her, it's the humidity. So different from dry Delhi …

For her second Instagram Reel, she wants to cover a famous Ros Omelette stall on Saligão Road. It shuts at 9.30 a.m., to open again at 3.30 p.m.—but the sun in Goa is too harsh during the afternoon hours. It will flatten her features and make her nose look like a potato. A ten-minute ride separates the *Dear Zindagi* road from the Saligão Road. Madhur stares angrily at her scooter, wondering if she should drag the useless thing home. What a waste of a Sunday it would be if she cannot shoot at least two Instagram Reels. As she deliberates her next move, a group of well-dressed people file out in an orderly manner from a nearby church.

Madhur had walked inside the same church's premises earlier, a beautiful old church called St. Anne's, but decided it deserved a lengthy vlog, not a reel.

The group of about thirty people—villagers from surrounding *vaddos* (village wards)—disperse after having attended the Sunday mass. Three young guys stay behind, loitering outside the church gates; they glance around to check if anyone's watching and then quickly light cigarettes. Staring at her in between puffs, they discuss something animatedly. Madhur kicks her scooter with more urgency. Suddenly, one guy stubs his cigarette and starts walking in her direction. She abandons her scooter and sprints down the coconut tree-lined road, as fast as her stilettoed-feet can take her, stopping only when she hears her scooter engine revving. Turning around she sees the guy waving at her, gesturing her to return. Sheepishly, Madhur walks back. What was she thinking, this is not Delhi. 'Thank you,' she says to him, 'and sorry I ran.'

'No problem,' he says and returns to his friends. As Madhur rides past them, they smile and wave. In her rear-view mirror, she sees them doubling over with laughter.

It's just been a week since Madhur arrived in Goa. She is a long way from understanding what makes the place and its people tick. She feels extremely safe here—except for stray coconuts trying to kill her. She can walk around wearing next to nothing, and the locals don't bat an eyelid. Not even the old grandmothers and grandfathers. And yet there is something about the place that she can't quite put a finger on, and that irks her.

Always smiling, always ready to help, the locals behave like they have no worries in the world. She wonders if that's possible.

Take for instance, when the rest of the country is reeling from COVID-19, but in Goa, everyone's making Instagram Reels.

No. That would be the tourists, Madhur corrects herself. Tourists like her, desperately wanting what the Goans have, with no clue how to get it. Or even what 'it' is.

CHAPTER 2

Kalkaji to Panaji[1]

Madhur Chopra had a YouTube channel called 'Madfashions' back in 2014, when she joined National Institute of Fashion Technology (NIFT), New Delhi, to study fashion design. Actually, she was a regular on YouTube since 2010, starting at the age of twelve, so by the time she enrolled in the fashion school, she was already a pro. Her classmates at NIFT laughed at her obsession—it was early days for social media. For Madhur, YouTube was her online diary—a storage platform to which she uploaded her class projects and her fashion experiments, with a videocam that had direct video/photo upload facility to Facebook and YouTube.

There was no concept of followers back then. Most people used YouTube to trim down family videos to 5MB files—the Facebook upload limit in those days. It was merely a feeder service for social media, and the videos just hung around on a page, for friends and family to see and leave comments.

---

1 Panjim is also known as Panaji.

Madhur's earliest videos had her modelling her own dresses on a *barsati* (terrace) or in a public garden. Her classmates left snarky comments on her videos:

> **SouthDelhiDiva:** *Kalkaji ki duplicate Gucci ko dekho!* (Look at Kalkaji's imitation Gucci!)
> **QueenYass:** Madhur thinks she's designing clothes for Madonna[2]!
> **SouthDelhiDiva:** Like, a virgin collection? Haaaw, nobody will touch!!!

It was before the term 'trolling' was invented, so she just grinned and ignored it.

Madhur Chopra's classmates at NIFT were from the upper echelons of New Delhi—their families owned franchises of retail fashion stores or bespoke haute couture boutiques. They lived either in Gulmohar Park, Greater Kailash or Panchsheel Enclave, hung out at Hauz Khas, Shahpur Jat and Khan Market, and watched FTV like the rest of the country watched cricket.

Madhur lived in Kalkaji, in a LIG (low-income group) colony. Her father was an insurance agent at the Life Insurance Corporation of India (LIC) office in Kalkaji. He had to take a loan for her to join NIFT. Dinkar Chopra, Madhur's father, was supportive of her career choice, unlike her mother, Damayanti Devi, who wanted her to study B.Com. or B.Sc. and also join

---

[2] This is a reference to the singer Madonna, known for her crazy fashion sense and the song, 'Like a virgin'.

LIC, or some other government office. But Dinkar Chopra was aware of the lucrativeness of India's fashion industry. 'Béta, design wedding dresses. *Bahut paisa hai usmé!* (There's a lot of money to be made!)' he would urge her.

Madhur was least interested in designing Indian-style wedding dresses. She was obsessed with beachwear and loungewear—quite unusual for a land-locked Delhi girl, who had never felt sand between toes. Her predilection for whisper soft fabrics and her penchant for pastel colours made her an oddity in a milieu defined by heavy zardozi. Her own mother would look at her creations—minimalistic in design as well as fabric—and cry, '*Hai méri maa!* Who'll wear these? Can a girl step out in Delhi wearing your clothes?'

'Maa, the girls who'll wear them have chauffeur-driven cars. They don't walk on Delhi streets,' Madhur would reply, defiantly. 'And it's meant for Bali and Maldives, not your Lajpat Nagar Market.'

At her final year graduation showcase, called 'Preview', Madhur was allotted the lower rung models—all 5 feet 7 inches tall, even though she had explicitly asked for taller girls. Her richer classmates called in favours from the top rung models—with whom they socialized regularly. 'Why do *they* need the six-foot girls?' Madhur had pleaded with her professors, 'Their wedding outfits will look better on shorter models. How many Delhi girls of marriageable age are 6 feet tall and weigh 45 kgs?' she demanded to know.

Madhur's loungewear collection fell flat on the catwalk. Her last-minute jugaad to make it fit on the assigned models, ended up ruining the drape and fall of her outfits. The judges tut-tutted in the first row. Her classmates giggled in the wings …

Madhur did not receive any offers from fashion houses and had to settle for a visual merchandiser's job at a mall in Saket; in charge of in-store displays, window displays and atrium installations.

One day, the sportswear showroom manager at the mall asked her to stay back after work. Some people from an ad agency were keen to meet her. Madhur was introduced to a young film executive and an older art director. The two ladies complimented her on her edgy, beach-themed window displays for their brand's 2018 Summer collection and enquired if she would style an ad film. They offered to pay her ₹1.5 lakh a day, for a two-day shoot, plus conveyance and food.

Madhur made a quick calculation. It was just two months since she had joined the mall, and at her current salary it would take her another six months to earn ₹3 lakh. Madhur said 'yes' to the ad agency people, executing a seamless jump from visual merchandising to styling ad films. And this is how Madhur Chopra became Maddie Chopra in the Delhi advertising circles, a newly recruited fashion stylist with an edgy aesthetic.

What followed was a hectic schedule of styling ad films and press shoots daily for almost two years, with no breaks even on Sundays. By December 2019, Madhur had earned enough money to buy her own boutique in the hip Shahpur Jat enclave. She spent the next two months designing and creating her first line of 'Madfashions', while Dinkar Chopra scouted for a boutique. Madhur fell in love with a tiny shop space. When they were about to finalize its sale deed, on 25 March 2020, the country went into a lockdown. And once again, Madhur's loungewear dreams came to naught.

The world in its entirety got cancelled, with paranoia surrounding the very air people breathed—which was highly polluted in Delhi to begin with. Human touch had to be avoided at all costs—which in Delhi, became a blessing for most women. Madhur was sequestered at home, finding solace in the fact that the universe wasn't unfairly singling her out this time. And besides, after two years of working full throttle, with no breaks whatsoever, this enforced inactivity was just what the doctor would have ordered.

The panic of the COVID-19's first wave subsided, and Dinkar Chopra started stepping out of the house. The LIC offices remained shut, but the agents were in demand as people rushed to get insured. He and other enterprising agents capitalized on people's pandemic-fuelled paranoia.

In May 2021, Dinkar Chopra died of COVID-19. He had never thought of insuring himself. All his savings were wiped out by hospital expenses, along with Madhur's boutique fund. She was left with a couple of lakhs.

At the cremation, Mehnaaz—the art director who had given Madhur her first styling break—whispered a brilliant idea. 'Become a fashion influencer, Maddie! Sell your outfits on Instagram and Facebook—malls and boutiques aren't opening for another year,' she said, as a handful of family members and friends watched the flames consume Dinkar Chopra's mortal remains.

Madhur whispered back, 'How can I sell clothes without knowing measurements, without doing fittings?'

'Maddie! It's how everyone's buying and selling clothes today!' Mehnaaz said, exasperatedly. Several heads turned to glare at them. 'If they don't fit, people return them. But you know how women are, they keep the clothes and try to lose weight instead!'

'Of course, you'll need to create elaborate images, with models and styling—easy-peasy for you. Would be wonderful if you could do it at a hill station resort, a beach resort or something,' Mehanaz continued. 'You know, locations are crucial for a fashion influencer—the more unusual the better.'

'*Sab kuch bund hai!* (Everything's shut!)' Madhur said dejectedly.

'You know what? Go to Goa! So many of my advertising friends are living there, in their holiday homes—everybody has WFH (work from home). Go live in Goa for a few months. Model your clothes in different settings. Sell your entire fashion line and only then return to Delhi—at least you'll make some money. Right now, it's just locked in those outfits.'

'Actually, that's not a bad idea, Mehnaaz … "Maddie Vlogs from Goa"? *Haan? Sahi hain?* (Right? Sounds right?)'

'Sounds perfect.' Mehnaaz urged her, 'Go and make Chopraji proud. Don't let his death be in vain; he totally believed in you.'

CHAPTER 3

Almost Famous

'*Bhaiyaa, ék Ros omelette kitné ka hai?* (Brother, how much for a Ros omelette?)' she asks the food-cart owner. A group of labourers turn around and stare at her. Madhur gets irritated, 'Side *do*,' she says to them curtly and moves closer to the cart.

'Which one you want, madam?' the middle-aged man asks her, plating omelettes and pouring ladles of curry on top. His son, standing beside him, sprinkles fistfuls of chopped onion and coriander garnish on top of each plate and serves the labourers. 'We have chicken Ros omelette, fish Ros omelette, mutton Ros omelette, chicken liver roll and shawarma.'

She peers inside three earthen pots containing curries in three different colours—mustard yellow, dark brown and orangish red; they smell different too. It's time for her sales pitch. 'Omelette-walle Bhaiyaa, my name is Madhur. I'm a famous fashion influencer and travel blogger—'

He interrupts her, 'I'm Peter, don't call me "Omelette-walle Bhaiyaa".'

'Sorry Bhaiyaa—I mean Peter, so, *jaisa mein bol rahi thi* (as I was saying), I want to shoot a video of your Ros omelette stall for my Instagram and YouTube channels. I have 50,000 followers. Your stall will become famous!'

He ponders over her spiel, flipping four omelettes on a large skillet, and wiping his sweaty brow with his free hand. His son whispers something, Peter shushes him. 'Means, you'll put video on internet?' he asks Madhur.

'Yes!' she says triumphantly, relieved that he comprehends her proposal.

His son meanwhile pulls out an iPhone from his trouser pocket. 'What's your channel called?'

'I have two channels—"Maddie Vlogs from Goa" and "Madfashions",' she says and waits as he scrolls.

'*Soglém Dilli videos, murrey!* (All Delhi videos, man!) Only five from Goa,' he says to his dad. 'Useless!'

'Useless?' Madhur asks angrily, 'I just came here a week ago. I'll make more videos, just wait and see. Then you'll feel bad you didn't get a video on "Maddie Vlogs from Goa" …'

Peter scolds his son and, looking apologetically at Madhur, he asks, 'Why you will put my video on internet? What you want?' Before she can respond he says, 'I give no money, okay?'

Madhur swallows hard, 'Okay, Peter. For you, no money. I will shoot a video of you making the dishes, then I'll interview you, and I'll eat every dish.'

'Madam, looking at your size only I'm telling you—you will not finish even one Ros omelette, forget roll and shawarma.'

'I will taste little-by-little and take the rest home.'

'Okay then, ₹350 for five items.'

'No, no, Bhaiyaa, *aap samjhé nahin* (you didn't understand) —sorry, Peter. You give free. Because I'm putting the video on internet,' she points to her phone screen, 'then my followers will come and eat here.'

'50,000 people?' he asks.

'Not that many, but 500 for sure.'

'Tomorrow?'

'No, slowly, slowly, over a month.'

'Héhh! I get more than that every week,' he tells her. 'I close shop now. You buy or not?'

'Peter Bhaiyaa, please! Please, please, Peter Bhaiyaa!'

'*Dii ré tekkām! Bheek magum yetām hi kalavantām, khoi saakun deo zanna!* (Give her! God alone knows from where these drama queens come, to beg over here!),' Peter starts shouting. His son starts packing rolls and omelettes on the double, while Madhur cowers, wondering if she should run again.

'Take,' the son hands her a largish parcel.

'Interview?' she asks.

'*Gharra vocch!* Go home!' shouts Peter.

A terrified Madhur slings the parcel on her scooter's handlebar and zips away. She reaches Almeida vaddo in Parra and parks outside Casa Coutinho. Her landlady, Mrs Coutinho, is watering the plants in her garden. 'Back from your morning ride?' she asks sweetly. 'Want breakfast?'

'No Auntyji, I got breakfast—lots.' Madhur opens the parcel to show her and remembers the coconut in her boot. She opens the boot and gives it to Mrs Coutinho, 'For your prawn curries,' she says.

'What for? So many coconuts we have! And what is this outside food? Tch tch, don't eat it! You'll fall sick, my child. Stomach upset you'll get!'

'Best Ros omelette in Goa,' Madhur says delightedly and runs to keep it in the kitchen. 'Can I use these blue and white Chinese-type plates for my video?' she calls out to Mrs Coutinho.

'No dear, don't touch them. They're from Macau,' Mrs Coutinho shouts to be heard.

'Auntyji! What is the use of keeping plates in showcase only?' Madhur laughs and goes to change her sweaty, icky dress. She picks out a pale lavender, fitted satin gown with spaghetti straps from her wardrobe. Wrapping a floral organza stole around her neck, she places her expensive Dior sunglasses on her head and dabs a bit of compact. After applying a hint of lip gloss, she is ready. Madhur steals a glance in the wardrobe mirror and runs to the kitchen. Opening the display cupboard, she takes the blue and white chinaware to the garden and lays it on grass near a large mango tree.

Mrs Coutinho is awestruck by Madhur's gown, and how beautiful she looks in it. Forgetting her earlier protests, she watches intently—hosepipe held in hand—at Madhur arranging food on her fine chinaware from Macau.

Madhur sees something amiss on her mobile screen and frowns. She stretches an arm to the rose bushes close by and plucks a rose—ignoring Mrs Coutinho's protests—and sprinkles the bright red petals around the plates. Satisfied, she takes the shot, and immediately uploads it to Instagram.

'Auntyji, ready?'

'Why you didn't tell me, I would've also worn a nice new dress,' Mrs Coutinho complains, feeling embarrassed of the frumpy house dress she's wearing. 'I didn't go to church today, or I too would be wearing my Sunday best.'

'Auntyji, why did you miss Sunday Mass? I was shooting near the church this morning,' Madhur says, putting an arm around Mrs Coutinho.

'Oh, I couldn't go. There's so much to do. Today is my orphanage day. First Sunday of every month I go to an orphanage in Thivim. I've been doing it for many years now. I help out the nuns and the children there. I cook, clean and sometimes I sew and fix torn clothes for them.'

'Wow, Auntyji! You do such noble work, I am inspired by you ... *lekin abhi ek reel banana hain* (but now we have to make a reel)!'

Switching to selfie mode she starts shooting.

MADHUR: Hello friends, I'm Madhur, and this is my most favourite person in Goa! Mrs Coutinho Auntyji. She is so awesome, *main kya bolun* (what can I say)! *Yeh dékho, kitni cute si hain na?* (See, isn't she cute?) Hai na osssumm? (Isn't she awesome?) By the way, Auntyji *ka naam kaafi* interesting hai. (Auntyji's name is very interesting.) Goa mein, after marriage, *ladies apna original surname bhi rakhtey hain.* (In Goa, after marriage, ladies retain their original surname.) So, Auntyji's full name is—

Madhur gestures to Mrs Coutinho to reply.

MRS COUTINHO: Marlena Mabel Pinto Coutinho.

Madhur switches to back camera and puts her mobile on a tripod.

MADHUR: So today I'm going to show you Goa's favourite street snack. *Isséy kéhtéy hain* Ros Omelette. (This is called Ros Omelette.) Basically, it's an omelette, *jiské uppar chicken, mutton, ya macchi ki gravy failaatéy hain* (it is covered with either chicken, mutton or fish gravy/ curry). It is then garnished with chopped onions and coriander. Let's taste it.

Madhur scoops a spoonful and eats it.

MADHUR: Mmmm, so tasty! *Mazaa aagaya!* I'm loving it! Friends, this is the yummiest thing you can eat on a Sunday morning in Goa. Simply awesome!

She turns to Mrs Coutinho, who is smiling shyly at the camera.

MADHUR: So Auntyji, tell me about these Chinese plates.

MRS COUTINHO: It is chinaware from Macau.

MADHUR: Macaw? *Matlab* (meaning), parrot?

MRS COUTINHO: No, no. Macau was a Portuguese colony, and my husband's family had businesses there for three generations.

MADHUR: See friends, every Goan-Portuguese house has *itihaas* (history)! And they are filled with so many antiques. Okaay! That's all I have for you today. This is 'Maddie Vlogs from Goa', signing out. Love you all, muaah! Like, subscribe, and keep those comments coming. Byeee!

Madhur folds her tripod, picks the plates and goes inside the kitchen. This is the sixth time she hasn't made any money in Goa. Shop owners, restaurant owners—why, even a street vendor—treat her like a beggar. She's a blogger, not a beggar, but when will they understand the difference? Hopefully some subscriber will like her outfit soon and place an order.

'Madhur dear, I have something to tell you,' Mrs Coutinho says, looking tense.

'*Haanji*, Auntyji, *batao?* (Yes, Auntyji, tell me?)'

'My daughter in the UK is complaining, because I gave you room with no security deposit.'

'I'm so grateful, Auntyji. I'll pay rent on time. *Aap fikar na karéy.* (Please don't be worried.)'

'Also, Stella, my daughter, she's saying I should keep distance. She saw you hugging me on a video, and she says not to bring street food inside the house because—'

'Already? She saw my video in UK *already*? I just uploaded it! See! I'm famous, I told you, na!' Madhur hugs Mrs Coutinho and runs to her room to edit her videos.

'Madhur! Lunch is already cooked. Serve yourself, okay? I'll be back home late in the evening,' Mrs Coutinho calls after her.

CHAPTER 4

#BestLife

'Goa in the rains is paradise on earth!' The tourism brochures were filled with such promises, tantalizing Madhur with pristine white sand beaches. She had imagined a turquoise blue ocean lapping on the shore, visible from an infinity pool. Palm fronds whispering as they fanned her fair skinned body moulded into a red-sequined Madfashions' swimsuit, stretched languorously on a white sunbed. One of her best designs, that swimsuit was not meant for swimming, but for flaunting at the poolside of a beach resort or villa. Raindrops would pitter-patter on her forehead, as she sipped an appletini. She would post the photos and the videos on all her social media accounts, with hashtags such as: #goalife #bestlife #livingthedream #Madfashions #swimsuits

But villas with infinity pools overlooking the ocean were a million miles outside Madhur's budget. Only Mrs Coutinho's crumbling mansion—seven kilometres from Calangute Beach, and eight kilometres from Anjuna, surrounded by mango trees and a vast coconut plantation—was affordable. And only because the large-hearted Mrs Coutinho had waived off her security deposit. As for the turquoise blue sea in Goa? Those photos were edited on either Photoshop or Lightroom.

Madhur wakes up and shuts off the alarm on her mobile. She immediately starts reading the DMs and comments on her Instagram page. As she's scrolling through her Facebook feed, she notices the clothes laid out neatly on a chair beside the bathroom door and sheepishly remembers why she had set the alarm. She runs to the bathroom to get dressed and skips out in five minutes wearing a red shirt tucked in a short denim skirt, her long poker-straight hair twisted loosely into a bun. Two foldable light reflectors of white and gold cloth, a selfie ring, tripod, adapters, extension cords and battery-operated spotlights are laid out on a study table. Thinking quickly, she ditches the spotlights, packing the rest of the equipment in her backpack. Opening Google Maps on her mobile, she feeds in her destination and runs out of the house to her scooter.

It's 5.30 a.m. and still quite dark when she arrives at the tableland hill of Vagator. Her destination, Ozran Beach, is down below. Narrow pathways, cutting through shrubs on the hill slope, go down to the beach. Wondering if it's safe to climb down in the dark, she switches on her mobile flashlight to navigate. Rocky boulders cover the entire beach, and she can hear the roar of waves crashing against them. After reaching the beach, she perches over the highest boulder and waits for sunrise.

As orange streaks start forming over the eastern horizon, Madhur gets up and starts looking for something between the boulders. Her mobile flashlight reveals a swarm of tiny black crabs with sharp red claws, scuttling around her feet; they duck into boulder crevices the moment she comes within crushing distance. From online pictures, Madhur knows that the beach is filled with black rocks and a small sandy area. But nobody said anything about crabs or sharp barnacles on those rocks. Clad in open-toed yellow flip-flops, she winces as the barnacles lacerate the sides of her feet. Salty sea waves washing over the cuts, sting sharply. She looks in all directions but can't seem to find it. If her mobile is to be believed, she's standing right on top of it. Getting down on her knees, she peers closely at the boulder below. Then, she sees it! A boulder carved into the shape of Lord Shiva's head. But the Shiva head is buried in sand up to its nose.

Madhur is aghast—it looks nothing like the online pictures. 'Same height as me!' she says aloud. She somehow thought it would be bigger—maybe she is confusing it with another Shiva statue … What images she had created in her mind! 'There's no way I can put this half Shiva head on my Insta feed,' she mutters to herself. *'Hai, ab kya karoon?* (Damn, what do I do now?)' Jumping down into the sand, she rolls up her sleeves and starts frantically digging the area around the carving's nose. If only she had carried something—like a plastic plate or a tumbler—she could have displaced the sand faster. After fifteen minutes, she unearths just a few inches more of his nose.

It's 6.00 a.m. now, and she is afraid the soft morning light will soon dissipate. She digs furiously, sweat darkening the armpits of her red shirt. The waves rushing in are compacting the sand, making it more and more difficult to dig. Just then she hears voices coming from the shoreline. Madhur stands up to see three fishing canoes coming in from the sea, with groups of strong men pulling them towards the only sandy part of Ozran Beach. Without thinking, she runs to the boats, waving at the fishermen—who look curiously at her and whisper amongst themselves. An old fisherman picks out two large pomfrets from his catch and gestures to a young boy to give them to her. 'No, no, I need help. I want to take photo beside Shiva head. But there's sand up to his nose. Can you help me dig?' she asks, 'Please, please help me!'

'*Amchi kama sodun hyaaka help korum?* (Stop our work and help her?)' one fisherman mutters under his breath, and all the others laugh. Madhur doesn't understand what's so funny, but seeing that they aren't budging, she tries again, 'Please, fisherman bhaiya!'

The old fisherman frowns, 'We're busy. Can't see?'

Madhur remembers something Mrs Coutinho often says, especially when she needs help with something. '*Por favor?* (Please?)' she says hesitantly, hoping she got the Portuguese pronunciation right.

Six able-bodied fishermen immediately stand up with their wooden oars. Madhur runs quickly towards the Shiva head, smiling at the irony of her situation. If this was any other place than Goa, she'd be a damsel in distress, fleeing a bludgeoning.

As the men start digging with their oars, Madhur fixes a ring light in front of her mobile and readies her frame. In just five minutes, the fishermen excavate the base of Shiva's head. Taking off her denim skirt and her red shirt, she reveals a red Madfashions swimsuit underneath. She climbs on the carved boulder. 'I need you to hold my reflectors,' she says, singling

out two tall fishermen, and gesturing them to stand close by her side—but outside her picture frame. Sitting in a lotus pose over the head, she clicks pictures by pressing a Bluetooth device, expertly concealed inside her hand mudra. The reflectors paint her body with a golden aura, highlighting the sequins on her swimsuits and making her skin glow.

After taking a few photos, Madhur jumps down to check her shots. The two fishermen are also curious to see the outcome. They look suitably impressed as she shows them the photos on her mobile. A few angle changes and fifteen minutes later, she wraps up by taking pictures of the fishermen, even as they protest.

The old fisherman requests for a group photo of all the fishermen with Madhur in the centre. He sends the young boy to fetch something, while Madhur is rigging the tripod for a wider group photo. The boy returns with pieces of checked red cloth. 'This is our traditional attire, we don't wear it now—except on special occasions,' the old fisherman tells her. Then, the ten fishermen strip behind rocks and step out wearing just red loin cloths. 'People feel embarrassed seeing our bums in this,' he says and guffaws. 'But I'm sure you won't mind. You are also dressed same-to-same,' he says giving her a toothless grin. They all strike poses—ten taut, suntanned bodies, in contrast with her fair feminine body.

Madhur looks at her photos and is stunned. How effortlessly all the elements of good photography—namely light, colour, composition and contrast—have come together so well. Serendipitously perfect shots—they are the Instagram gold she always hopes to mine, but rarely succeeds. It dawns on her that the best photos happen not by planning, but by being at the right place at the right time and seizing the moment.

The old fisherman retrieves his mobile wrapped inside a plastic bag and asks her to share the group pictures via Bluetooth.

'You'll put photo on newspaper?' he asks her.

'No,' Madhur replies sheepishly, 'I'll put on internet.'

'Internet better than newspaper,' he says, giving her a thumbs up sign.

As she is packing her equipment, the old fisherman offers her the pomfrets again. This time, Madhur accepts. Mrs Coutinho will be happy, she thinks.

'Obrig-obrig …' she tries to remember another word that Mrs Coutinho uses.

'*Obrigado* (Thank you),' the old fisherman says with a wide smile.

'Haan! *Obrigado*-ji!' she repeats.

Madhur climbs up to where her scooter is parked, and suddenly it starts to rain heavily with sharp pelting drops. But it doesn't bother her. In fact, she is delighted to ride in the first torrential showers. She has only experienced short drizzles so far, due to a delayed monsoon in Goa this year. Barely five minutes later, as she's cruising at 20kmph, a bus suddenly halts in front of her, without warning. Madhur brakes immediately, but despite her best efforts to save herself, she falls down and suffers bruises.

The bus conductor steps out and starts abusing her in Konkani. Madhur is fuming too. 'How would I know that your driver was going to stop so suddenly? And without giving a signal… you think I can read people's minds kya?' She asks angrily. An old gentleman trailing her, and having seen what transpired, stops and takes her side. He sternly warns the conductor with a police complaint. The conductor bolts and the bus drives away as if nothing happened. Madhur is astonished—not by the accident—but by the fact that someone actually stopped and helped. She didn't expect anyone to take a woman's side, especially in a road accident. She thanks the gentleman and continues riding to Parra.

It suddenly strikes her that she did not record the accident on her phone! She could have put it on her vlog, with the caption: *Goa ke nalayak bus conductors.* (Goa's careless bus conductors). It would have made for valuable advice on what to expect on Goa's roads. And it definitely would've gotten tons of likes and views—accident videos always do. Perhaps more than her morning's photoshoot. Meanwhile, it has stopped raining, and the breeze has dried her clothes. As Madhur enters the Almeida vaddo lane, she spots Mrs Coutinho standing on the road and arguing animatedly with a scooterist. She is constantly pointing inside a blue plastic crate attached to his scooter. Madhur pulls up closer and realizes that it's a fish vendor. She parks her scooter on the side of the road and runs to her. 'Coutinho Auntyji, I have fish! Don't buy!' she shouts excitedly, waving the fish wrapped in newspaper. 'Here,' she says, handing it to Mrs Coutinho, whose eyes pop out and jaw drops on seeing their size. 'How much you paid for this? Must be a thousand each!' she scolds Madhur. Madhur smiles and says, 'Come inside, I'll tell you the whole story.'

'How much did you pay?' Mrs Coutinho repeats, as she follows Madhur inside to the kitchen. 'Nothing!' Madhur laughs delightedly and narrates her morning adventure at Ozran Beach. By the end of the story, Mrs Coutinho grins from ear to ear. 'You actually said "por favor" and "obrigado"? My own Stella refuses to speak Portuguese. By the way, you should say "obrigada". When a man says it, he will say "obrigado".'

'Oh, Portuguese words have gender, just like Hindi!' Madhur exclaims.

Noticing a torn patch on Madhur's right shoulder, Mrs Coutinho asks, 'How did you tear such a nice shirt? Give it to me, I'll fix it.' Madhur suddenly gets self-conscious, 'It's nothing Auntyji, even I know to stitch,' she says and rushes to her room, before the old lady spots anymore cuts and bruises inflicted by the accident.

Whilst changing her clothes, Madhur sees a big angry contusion on her right shoulder—the whole area is blue-black now. As the adrenaline has worn off, her shoulder feels like it's dislocated. But then, her arm would dangle or have shooting pain. Her shoulder only seems bruised, so, Madhur quickly recites the Hanuman Chalisa and gives thanks to God.

After dinner, she decides to post about her accident anyway—so what if she missed the opportunity to shoot it live? A late post works equally well, or, rather, some post is better than no post at all.

Lying on her bed, with only an ornate nightlamp beside her for a dramatic effect, Madhur pulls down one strap of her black silk negligee.

 **MADHUR:** Hey guys, it's me again, *aapki* Madhur. You must be wondering why I am looking *thodisi* (a little) depressed ... *Yeh dekho* (see) friends ...

She pushes her bare bruised shoulder provocatively into the frame.

MADHUR: *Aaj mere saath yeh hua!* (This happened to me today!)

She sees her viewer count jump from 50 to 200, and everybody is sending her bleeding hearts in the chat box.

MADHUR: I was riding on the Arpora Road, *aur ek baddi si bus achanak méré samné rukh gayi* (and a big bus halted suddenly in front of me).

One viewer sends her ₹1,000, with a super chat message begging her to show more skin.

MADHUR: *Toh aaj mainé bus ko thok diya!* (So I banged a bus today!)

Madhur says pouting. The chat goes wild, with comments and emojis flying at her in the chat box.

Aashik2000: *Mujhey bhi thok do! Bandaa haazir hain!* (Bang me too! I'm available!)

MADHUR: Okay, now for the serious part, always wear a helmet when you are riding your bike or scooter—*poorey India mein, aur definitely Goa mein* (in all of

India, and definitely in Goa). Guys, *yahaan ké bus driver rules follow nahin kartéy. Woh kahin bhi rukh jatey hain, especially beech sadak mein!* (The bus drivers over here do not follow any rules. They stop anywhere, without warning- especially in the middle of a street!)

She thinks for a moment, before continuing.

MADHUR: *Aur ek last ki baat* (and one last thing) … there are so many coconut trees in Goa. They look pretty, and nariyal-paani is very-very tasty, but beware of falling coconuts, they can kill you. One more reason you should always wear a helmet in Goa. That's it from me friends, *yahaan baarish jorron se shurru hogayi hain* (it's raining heavily here). It's the first week of July 2021. Like aur subscribe karein. *Aur paise bhi kabhi kabaar dé diya karein. Mujhey nayi scooter dilwa do please!* (And send me some money now and then. Get me a new scooter, please!) Joking guys! See you soon!

She looks at the video statistics and smiles. Accident videos definitely do well. Maybe she should buy a GoPro to strap on her forehead whilst riding, like the mountain bike riders. But it will look rather silly, and will, over time, leave a permanent mark on her forehead. No, she can't have that.

Next day, Mrs Coutinho's daughter in the UK sees the beach and accident videos, and calls her mother. 'Mummy, what kind of girl have you kept as a tenant?' she asks. 'Fashion influencer, my arse. Madhur is a porn star! You better keep somebody decent. Ask her to leave, right now. I can send you more money if you're finding it difficult to manage. No need to keep tenants.'

'It's not for money,' Mrs Coutinho says, wearily. 'I'm alone in this big house, I need company. And by the way, this is what all youngsters are doing in Goa,' she emphasizes. 'You're becoming old fashioned in the UK, I think,' Mrs Coutinho says wryly, and ends the call.

She confronts Madhur right away. 'You had accident yesterday and you didn't tell me? Told the whole world on internet—as if they can come out of your mobile phone and help you,' she scolds Madhur. 'Show me where you got hurt.'

'Oh Auntyji, it's nothing! See, so small, just a bruise,' Madhur says, pulling her T-shirt neck below her right shoulder.

'Madhur, get a car, no? Bikes are dangerous.'

'Okay Auntyji, I will get one when I make more money. Then we'll both go on long-long drives!'

'Yes, please! Just like my Godfrey used to take me, long, long ago,' Mrs Coutinho says, smiling warmly.

CHAPTER 5

Tall Glass of Russian

Madhur's laptop screen goes blank one morning. '*Hai Ram*, this monsoon humidity has screwed up its battery,' she says, and packs it in plastic inside her backpack. She heads out to Fiera Alta in Mapusa—many computer peripheral stores are located there.

The technician at a shop checks her laptop and says, 'Oh my god! Battery is bloated! Better change it right now.'

'Do it. I cannot survive without my laptop.'

'Your battery model is currently not in stock, but I can get it from our Panjim godown. It will take an hour. You can come back tomorrow,' he tells her.

'No, I'll wait here till you return.'

An hour is a long time to kill. She reads and re-reads all their brochures, surfs the internet on their display laptops. She's fantasizing about a laptop with a fast compressor—perfect for video editing—when all of a sudden there's a loud crash! She crouches down in time to avoid being showered by shattered glass. Madhur turns to look at the entrance and sees a tall, shirtless Russian man, sporting a buzz cut and dressed in a sarong. He is standing by the entrance, evidently entering the showroom by crashing through its glass door.

The store manager is shocked. The Russian looks like a hitman from a James Bond film, and he's muttering, '*Yakyak winner what! Yaktak winna wat?*' He repeats the phrase on a loop, whilst holding his head and looking at the shattered glass around him. Madhur gathers her wits and approaches him. 'Are you okay? Understand English? Speak English?' she asks.

'Yes, yes. Sorry, sorry,' he says. 'See no glass door.'

The store manager comes over with a glass of water. 'No problem, we'll fix the door … are you hurt, sir?'

'No hurt! Scratch,' he says.

'How can I help you? You want to buy laptop or computer?'

'No laptop. DTP design I want. See lady doing computer work,' he points to Madhur. 'Inside come, I … break glass. Sorry, *ya tak vinovat*.'

'Sir, the DTP shop is next door. We are a computer showroom.'

'I go next door. No unnerstand, no unnerstand! One hour waste, no unnerstand!' He gets agitated.

'Hi, I'm Madhur, I also do DTP design,' she introduces herself, sensing an opportunity. She wonders how Russians deal with the heat and humidity of Goa. When she was in school, many Russians came to Delhi during winter, to shop for clothes and handicrafts at Chandni Chowk, Connaught Place and Dilli Haat. They then sold them in their countries at ten times the original price. Now online shopping lets you buy cheap clothes and handicrafts from anywhere in the world, without stepping out of your house.

Before shifting to Goa, Madhur researched a lot about the state. She learnt that many from the fractured former Soviet states, had set up businesses in Goa, on the beaches of Ashwem, Mandrem and Morjim. They were the hippies of the new millennium, escaping their frigid, totalitarian countries for the warm freedom of Goa.

'I Ivan, hello!' the Russian says to Madhur. In his broken English, he explains to her that he wants a logo and a visiting card designed for his girlfriend's boutique on Morjim Beach. Madhur presumes that the DTP operators next door did not understand his heavily accented English, or his exacting standards.

'When do you want it?' she asks.

'Now,' Ivan says, and smiles.

Just then the technician arrives with her battery from the godown. The puzzled look on his face at seeing no glass door, reduces them all to peals of laughter.

'Okay, I can do it now,' Madhur says.

'Money?' Ivan asks her, gesturing with his thumb and forefinger.

'How much will you pay?' she asks. Madhur doesn't know design rates in Goa.

'₹2000 DTP shop. ₹3000 you.'

'Done,' Madhur says, opening Photoshop on her laptop. In fifteen minutes—with shirtless Ivan peering over her—

she draws a fashion illustration with her track pen, adds the boutique name in a clean font, and the logo is ready. In another five minutes, she designs a visiting card.

'Okay?' she asks. Ivan responds with a loud guffaw. Madhur looks a little worried as he continues snorting. Finally, he stops and says, '*O Bozhé! O Bozhé! Bozhe moy!*'

'What?' she asks. The manager looks at her and wonders aloud, 'Does he want bhajias?'

'O God, o my god, this goot,' Ivan says, giving her a thumbs up. He pulls out a USB from his wallet. Madhur transfers the files, but holds on to the USB, hesitating to hand it over.

'*Yak tak vinowat,*' he says again, and fishes out a bundle of 500 notes from his fanny pack. He gives her some, he gives her a lot more than he promised.

'Ivan, this is ₹6,000. Too much,' Madhur says to him.

'Keep,' he says, 'You designer. Same to same my girlfriend. Goot!' he makes a thumbs up sign again. He points to her mobile and says, 'Give.' He types his number into her contacts. 'Call,' he says. 'Work lots, boutique December open.'

'Ivan, may I take picture and shoot a small video?' she asks hesitantly.

'Yes, yes,' he says, blue eyes twinkling. As Madhur stands beside him, he bends his knees to come down to her height. She puts one arm around his wide shoulders and goes live on social media.

 **MADHUR:** Hello friends, myself Madhur Chopra, and this is Ivan. Ivan, your full name?

IVAN: Ivan Kuznetsov, me Russia. Love Goa!

He smiles to the camera and does a heart sign.

MADHUR: Ivan is my new friend in Goa. I just made a design for him—no, not an outfit, a logo design. I'm sure ki we will be seeing each other more. Na, Ivan? More about Ivan later, *woh zaraa jaldi mein hain* (he is in a hurry). Ivan, say 'Like and subscribe'.

IVAN: Like, subscribe Madurai channel! Madurai goot designer!

MADHUR: Dasvidanya, Ivan!

IVAN: Ho ho! Dasvidanya, Madurai.

Madhur rides home feeling the same emotions she had felt when she bagged her first advertising assignment—even though the payment is much smaller this time. Maybe, apart from vlogging, she can also pursue graphic design in Goa. Though it might be a great opportunity if she could keep some of her outfits at Ivan's girlfriend's boutique. But she has seen those shack-like beach boutiques; they offer bargains below ₹5,000, sometimes below ₹1,000 even. Meant for backpackers, their beachwear can hardly be classified as 'Haute Couture'. Right now, she is just eager to get home and tell Mrs Coutinho of her encounter with the shirtless Russian.

CHAPTER 6

Everybody's Vloggin'

August comes to an end, and Goa is cloaked in myriad hues of green. Laterite stone walls of houses have turned a dark mossy green. Rice fields are a swaying mass of lemon green. And creepers cover everything with a blanket of viridian green, climbing over trees, houses and electric poles—even weaving their delicate tendrils around powerlines.

The lockdown is lifted, and new restaurants are opening every day, even in small villages. More people are visiting Goa than ever before—all those who would normally vacation in Thailand, Malaysia, Maldives, Mauritius or Sri Lanka, are coming to Goa. What's even worse is that those who would go to Aruba, Ibiza or Santorini, are also coming to Goa, due to restrictions on international travel. And then, there are the regulars, who just love the state anyway.

Goa has unwittingly become a mecca for influencers. Every second person on the road, beach or restaurant, is a self-proclaimed 'famous influencer', capturing Goa through a mobile screen. Everybody is demanding money for reviewing restaurants, hotels and boutiques, in lieu of views and promotion.

Madhur looks at them and thinks, *Arré O Samba, kitnéy followers thay? Ek lakh sé zyaada, huzoor!* (O Samba, how many followers were there? More than a lakh, lord!)

The models with their never-ending legs are here, rich kids with their daddy's Mercs are here, cricketers with their physios are here, Bollywood A-listers with their entourages are here—what chance does 'Maddie Vlogs from Goa' stand?

'Thank God, Auntyji, I came here in June, in the middle of the pandemic. Look at the crowd now! In just two months Goa is a completely different place. I hate going out—wherever I go, I bump into someone I know! All my snooty classmates are here,' Madhur tells Mrs Coutinho one afternoon. 'And, when they see me, they immediately look away. They don't want to acknowledge me! Can you believe it—the rich and the middle-class are all hanging out at the same places in Goa? Same restaurants, same pubs!'

'You please don't eat at those restaurants. What will I do with the food I cook for you? Tie it around your neck?'

'*Arré no*, Auntyji, don't worry! I can't eat out now. All these rich people have pushed the prices of everything through the roof. Even the Ros Omelette guy in Saligāo has increased his rates,' Madhur says dejectedly.

As other bloggers and vloggers concentrate on Goa's outward beauty, Madhur decides to turn inward—to show a different, rarely seen (by non-Goans, that is) side of Goa to her viewers. She has access to such a place, only because she stays in an old crumbling mansion with a local. Casa Coutinho—though devoid of modern conveniences like ACs, microwave, food processors and geysers—has a cornucopia of antiques in its cavernous interiors.

Madhur's latest vlogs focus on Goan customs, traditional home-cooked food, architecture and indigenous fabrics. Her guide is her ebullient landlady, Mrs Coutinho. The old woman has overcome her initial shyness and actively participates in Madhur's shenanigans—in fact, she leads them now, using the videos and photoshoots as an excuse to show-off her stately heirlooms or her singing prowess. Every other video, in addition to a gorgeously attired Madhur, also features Mrs Coutinho in a formal gown or an elegant silk sari, her silver-grey hair styled with a rose or a hibiscus flower from her garden.

'Auntyji, sit on this,' Madhur says, directing the old lady to an antique maroon velvet chaise lounge that has faded over the years. Madhur makes a mental note to brighten the velvet with filters. Mrs Coutinho sits on the chaise lounge, dressed in a pale green silk sari with intricate gold embroidery.

'Wah, Auntyji! You look just like Waheeda Rehman,' Madhur exclaims, looking through her mobile. 'Now, say something!'

> **MRS COUTINHO:** What to say … okay, I'll tell you about this sari. Silk is from Macau—Godfrey's family did business there, I told you, na? So, my father-in-law used to order bales of silk and satin fabric for me, to stitch gowns and dresses. I liked this one so much, I didn't want to cut it up, so I turned it into a sari, and did the embroidery myself, by hand! I wore it for my sister's wedding—she got married two years after me.
>
> *Suddenly, Mrs Coutinho breaks into a lilting Portuguese song. Madhur is transfixed. It sounds like something out of an opera—not that she's ever been to one.*
>
> **MRS COUTINHO:** *Numa casa portuguesa fica bem,*
>   *pão e vinho sobre a mesa.*
>   *e se à porta humildemente bate alguém,*
>   *senta-se à mesa co'a gente …*[3]
>
> *Mrs Coutinho stops singing, feeling emotional after the first stanza.*

---

3 In a Portuguese house it is good to have
bread and wine on the table.
and if someone humbly knocks on the door,
we invite him to sit at the table with us…
Song by Amália Rodrigues (Portuguese actress, known as the queen of fado)

MRS COUTINHO: I sang this fado at my sister's wedding. It's called "Uma Casa Portuguesa", which means "a Portuguese house". I sang it to wish my sister a happy married life.

Madhur's new videos have an archival feel, as if she were recording an important moment in time, showing to the world a Goa that will soon disappear. But strangely, her viewership is declining. Every new video gets fewer and fewer likes. Her beloved readers leave distasteful comments.

Aashik 2000: *Buddhi aurat mat dikhao yaar! Tu khud bikini pehen ké sofey par baith lio.* (Don't show the old woman! You sit on the sofa wearing a bikini.)

SexyRahul-99: *Auntyji ko apné jaghey rahené do, tu beach pé jaa!* (Let Auntyji stay at her own place, but you go visit a beach!)

Baby-Dollz: Not interested in seventy-year-old woman's life. I already have grandmother at home!

NerdyNaresh: Seriously disliking this channel …*yeh toh art film banané lagi* (she has started making some indie film)!

Altaf: *Hum vell'ley hain kya? Kuch zabardast content dikhwa dio.* (Are we sitting idle? Show us some exciting content.)

Madhur is confused by their reactions.

MaddievlogsfromGoa: Friends, I'm showing you the real Goa. The simple people, their culture. Goa is not

Everybody's Vloggin'

> just about boozy beach parties, you know. Yes, there is a culture of drinking here, but it's very refined. In fact, many people here make their own wines, traditionally, at home! My next video will be on that!
>
> **DilliRomeo:** No need! We have wine shops. Show us bikini babes on the beach!
>
> **MaddievlogfromGoa:** Hai Ram! Y'all will never change!

One day Mrs Coutinho challenges Madhur, 'You think only you have sexy gowns? Wait, I'll show you mine!' She pulls out a bundle from her wardrobe, a white wedding gown is wrapped inside it. Forcing Madhur to wear it, Mrs Coutinho is surprised at how perfectly it fits her. Madhur has the same delicate frame Mrs Coutinho had as a young bride in the 1970s. Her daughter, Stella, on the other hand, has a stocky athletic built, like her husband, Godfrey.

The once-white China silk has turned a pale yellow from being kept wrapped for fifty years. 'Stitched it myself on my Singer machine,' she tells Madhur, showing her a big wooden box in the bedroom corner.

'I also have a Singer machine at home, in Kalkaji, but it's not so big,' says Madhur as she walks up to it and lifts the top. '*Oi maa! Yeh to Baba Addam ké zamane ki machine hain!* (Oh dear! This machine is very old!)'

Mrs Coutinho gets the gist of what Madhur just said and laughs, 'I know, I know, but it's not that old also.' She gazes at it fondly, caressing its shiny black metal body secured atop a polished wooden table. It is a 1940s model with a foot pedal—it belonged to her mother and was handed down to her as part of her wedding trousseau. Opening the side drawers, she shows Madhur a stash of coloured threads, buttons, needles of different sizes and spare bobbins. Madhur is already filming with her mobile. 'Auntyji, did you do the embroidery on your wedding dress with this machine?' she asks, holding up the netted trail with one hand and showing it to Mrs Coutinho.

'No dear, I did this by hand. Machine cannot execute such delicate thread work.'

'*Dekha!* My machine is better than yours. Technology *bhi koi cheeze hoti hain!* (Technology has its own merits!) My machine is so advanced that it can do 250 types of embroidery patterns—some very delicate.' Madhur declares triumphantly.

'Okay baba! Yours is better than mine! Even Stella was forcing me to throw away this *khatara* (rusted machine) and get a hi-tech white Singer machine. But I said no.'

'Good you didn't, Auntyji. Technology is great, but it has no character. Your machine is a work of art. If I had this, I would just sit and admire it all day—forget about stitching anything. And my white machine … why do they always make everything white—fridges, computers, cars, ACs? *Jab nayi technology adopt kartey hain, toh sab cheezé white colour mein hi kyon banaatey hain?* (Whenever a new technology or device is introduced, why is it always in white?)'

'I think because white is pure and trustworthy. Like the wedding dress you're wearing,' Mrs Coutinho points out to her.

'*Haaaanh… sahi baat boli aap* (Yesss … you are right),' concurs Madhur. 'Do you still stitch your clothes on this?' she asks Mrs Coutinho, who is placing the wooden box cover back on the machine. 'Not like before. Nowadays I just use it for minor hemming and fixing torn clothes. Or turning torn clothes into dusters,' she replies sullenly.

'But you said you stitch for the kids at the Thivim orphanage.'

'I just repair their torn clothes now. I cannot stitch like before. Earlier I would stitch their uniforms, dresses, curtains, upholstery … Now I cannot see properly,' she declares. 'I'm afraid my fingers will get pricked under needle, get a nice cross stitch pattern on them,' she says and laughs. 'My tailor Amar in Jackhni vaddo stiches all my dresses now,' Mrs Coutinho admits, with a tinge of guilt. 'But when Stella was in college, I stitched all her dresses—even for her friends and their mothers. Nice pocket money I made! You know Madhur, I used to take orders for wedding dresses too. My Godfrey used to work late in his upstairs office, and I would stitch—sometimes till morning, waiting for him to finish work.'

'How sweet! Toh you are Parra's famous wedding dress designer!'

'What famous? My own daughter didn't let me stitch her a wedding dress. She went to UK to study and married an Englishman. Got herself a designer wedding gown,' Mrs Coutinho says ruefully. '"Don't want your old-fashioned gowns, mamma" she said over phone …'

Madhur stops filming and smiles, 'Auntyji, all young girls like designer clothes. *Unko sirf label chahiyé!* (They just want a famous label!) When she is old, na, then she'll appreciate hand-stitched stuff,' she says, smoothing down the pleats of Mrs Coutinho's gown. 'I love your wedding gown! So beautiful and simple it is …' says Madhur, observing herself in a full-length oval mirror with an ornate teakwood frame. 'I feel like a princess—no, a queen!'

'Let's find you a nice Goan boy!' Mrs Coutinho chuckles, observing Madhur.

'Oi maa! My mother will kill me! She wants me to marry in my *biradari*—my community. But I don't want to marry at all,' says Madhur.

'Why dear? I'm sure there's a line of boys waiting to marry you.'

'Even if there is, I won't like any boy standing in it,' Madhur speaks to herself in the mirror.

'Oh my! Choosy you're, my dear girl! It's good, but only up to a point, haan?'

'Auntyji, all the boys of my biradari are very different from me. Actually, I'm different from the girls of my biradari. The boys and girls are fine as they are, *mujhi mein* problem *hain* (the problem is in me),' says Madhur.

'What problem? There's no problem with you. Any boy should be lucky to marry you.'

'No Auntyji, those chomus behave like they are John Abraham! They'll stop me from doing things I like. No vlogging, no fashion design or getting my own boutique—which I will own, someday. I'll have to wear salwars and saris only. *Main mar jaoungi!* (I'll die!)'

'Madhur, if your community boys are backward, you should marry modern boys from another community.'

Madhur smiles, 'I wish you could talk to my mother, Auntyji. You're so much older than her, *par aapké vichaar kitné modern hain* (but you have such a modern outlook)!'

'I think I will speak to her. Let's send her your picture right now and say that you got married here in Goa. Isn't that what all you Delhi people like?' Mrs Coutinho winks at Madhur.

'Nahi, Auntyji! She won't understand a word of English or even your Hindi. Now show me that master bedroom, I have to make a *todu* (path-breaking) reel. I completely forgot, looking at your Baba Addam machine!'

Mrs Coutinho walks to the wooden staircase leading upstairs to the first floor. Madhur follows behind, gingerly holding up the precious wedding gown. As they climb up, they arrive at a large open study covered wall to wall with old hardbound books. The floor and walls are panelled in teakwood. There is a stately teakwood table, with a tall leather upholstered chair. Mrs Coutinho's late husband, Mr Godfrey Coutinho, was an advocate who practised at the Mapusa High Court. This study served as his office.

A long corridor from the study leads to Stella's bedroom and the couple's master bedroom. Both are locked. 'Very dusty dear … I don't go inside much,' Mrs Coutinho says, opening her master bedroom. She uses the smaller bedroom downstairs, next to Madhur's room. 'It's very dark inside, not good for video.'

'Let me see at least, Auntyji!'

The master bedroom has pale blue walls. Mellow light permeates through a large, frosted glass window, specs of dust visible in its path. All the furniture is covered with white cloth, giving the room an eerie feel. As Mrs Coutinho opens the window, branches of a mango tree rush inside immediately. She looks irritated, 'He never let me cut it, such a pain this tree is!'

'So cut it now, na,' Madhur says to her.

'No, he'll feel bad,' Mrs Coutinho replies.

'Auntyji, shall I remove these covers? Please?'

'Shi, shi, so much dust! My dress will get soiled,' she chides Madhur.

'Oh Auntyji, *sab kuch showcase mein, ya phir cover ké andar! Yeh kaisi zindagi?* (Oh Auntyji, either everything is inside cupboards or kept under covers! What kind of life is this?)'

'Haan haan, *Dear Zindagi*,' Mrs Coutinho says, referring to a Bollywood film that was shot close by, near her church. 'It wasn't like this when my Godfrey was alive. Everything was tip-top. My Godfrey liked everything clean, that's why I keep his office spic and span, even today.'

Madhur pulls off a huge white sheet covering a four-poster bed at the centre of the room. The bed is the size of a small room—a luxurious padded room. Mrs Coutinho opens a wardrobe and takes out a bundle of white gossamer soft fabric. She gestures to Madhur to place it above the bed posts. Madhur climbs on the bed and hangs it carefully, adjusting the length equally on all sides. Afterwards, she sits at the centre of the gossamer tent and fixes her mobile on the tripod. Now the four-poster bed looks like it is covered with a bridal veil, under whose canopy is seated a diminutive Madhur, also wearing a bridal gown.

Mrs Coutinho switches on the bedside lamps and a chandelier above the bed—it showers Madhur with a golden light, bathing her with resplendence. Mrs Coutinho sighs.

Madhur starts her live broadcast.

MADHUR: Hello my darlings, this is *aapki* Madhur, *urf* Maddie! Today I'm dressed as a Goan bride. Please note that this is NOT a Madfashions outfit and it's NOT for sale, because, *doston*, this is priceless! I'm wearing a vintage wedding outfit that belongs to Mrs Coutinho. This is how Goan brides dressed in 1970s!

Madhur stands on the bed and twirls two-three times in front of her tripod mounted mobile. She then flops down and holds her veil close to the mobile.

MADHUR: Yeh dekho, look at this detailing, this embroidery style, it is so, so...*nazuk* (delicate). *Abhi koi nahi karta aisi kaarigari* (nobody does this kind of detailed work any more)...

The comments start scrolling on her mobile screen.

Vanya95: Ooh super! I love vintage fashions ...

Ravi$: *Neck thodasa deep hota to achha hota. Khair, acchi lag rahi ho tum!* (If it had deeper neckline, then it would have been better. Still, you look nice!)

Goagirl89: My grandma wore a similar dress, I've seen in photos. Keep rocking Maddie. You show the real Goa!

Madhur quickly reads the live comments and smiles.

MADHUR: *Aur yeh* antique four-poster bed *toh dekho! Yeh* chandelier—*waisé* sitting room *mein iss sé kaafi bada* chandelier *hai.* (See this antique four-poster bed! And this chandelier—although the chandelier in the sitting room is bigger.)

Tony4U: *Main aata hoon, four-poster bed toodwané, mera bhi kaafi bada hogaya hai!* (I can come over to break-in the four-poster bed, mine has grown big too!)

Madhur picks up the mobile and pans the whole bedroom.

MADHUR: *Aaj sirf itna hi.* (That's it for today.) Before I go, everyone say hello to my darling Coutinho Aunty. She designed and stitched this dress! Okay byeee, everybody!

> **Romeoshomeo:** *Phir sé buddhi!* (Again the old woman!)
>
> **ViralVeer:** *Chudail hai woh! Sambhaal lio!* (She is a witch! Stay alert!)
>
> **Sweetypriya:** Cho cuteeee!
>
> **Row10_22:** Sweet you both are! Hello aunty!

Mrs Coutinho helps her out of the wedding gown. They lock the master bedroom and go downstairs, Madhur to her room to edit the longer videos, and Mrs Coutinho to the kitchen.

At dinner, Mrs Coutinho is not her usual talkative self. Madhur, too, is in a contemplative mood. Wearing the wedding dress seems to have stirred latent emotions in both. Madhur is not plied with the usual second helpings, as Mrs Coutinho hastily collects the plates and clears the dining table. 'Madhur dear, will you join me for prayers tonight, before you sleep?' she asks. Madhur is a little surprised by this request. 'As you wish, Auntyji,' she says. At 10.00 p.m., Madhur goes to Mrs Coutinho's bedroom, and finds her kneeling on the floor with her elbows on the bed, hands clasped around a rosary. Madhur joins her. Mrs Coutinho starts:

> Jesus Christ, my Lord, I adore you
> I thank you for all the graces you have given me this day.
> I offer you my sleep and all the moments of my night,
> I ask you to keep me without sin.

I place myself on your sacred side and under the mantle of our lady, my mother.
Let your angels stand above me and keep me in peace and your blessings be upon me.
Amen.

Madhur repeats 'Amen'—it's the one word she knows. And how to sign the cross—having seen both gestures in movies. Mrs Coutinho kisses her goodnight and climbs into bed. As Madhur walks to her room, she adds a few more lines to Mrs Coutinho's prayer.

'Please, Jesus Bhagwan, give me new subscribers. Grant my videos more views and likes. Let my clothes sell via Instagram and Facebook, dear bhagwan. Or I will have to seriously look for a job. Jesus Bhagwan aur Mary Maiyaa, *meri madat karo please* (please help me)! *Mujhé boutique, car, ya zyada paise nahin chahiyé* (I don't need a boutique, car or a lot of money) … just enough to get me through the day … and a new scooter will not hurt.'

CHAPTER 7

Gone in Two Seconds

Mrs Coutinho requests Madhur to go to the Panchayat office one morning, to pay the House Tax for their villa. 'Don't do your video-shideo! Just pay the money, take the receipt and come back home,' she instructs her.

Madhur sees a huge crowd inside the Panchayat premises, spilling onto the road, obstructing traffic. Parking her scooter, she asks someone, 'Film shooting?' They just shrug and continue gawking. She elbows her way through the crowd, saying, 'Side please!', 'Uncleji, side!' and 'Excuse me!' Finally, she reaches the entrance. A bouncer stops her, 'No autograph, no selfie,' he says. Madhur thinks, *Kya baat hain! Yeh Panchayat hain ya koi night club? Itna crowd, aur bouncer uncle bhi!* (What's the matter? Is this a Panchayat or a night club? There's so much crowd, including a bouncer uncle!) ... 'I have to pay my house tax, side do, bouncer uncle!' she says to the burly man. He immediately steps aside to let her pass.

Inside the sarpanch's glass cabin, a 1980s Bollywood star is holding adda. He is here to seek permission for an illegal extension to his Parra bungalow. Madhur wonders if she'll see money being passed under the table, then remembers Mrs Coutinho's warning; she stops staring and looks for the house tax counter. A clerk calls out to her and takes her payment. As she is about to leave, the superstar also walks out of the cabin and they both hesitate at the exit. '*Péhlé aap* (You first),' she says nervously. He makes eye contact and folds his hands dramatically, '*Nahinji, péhlé aap!* (No, you first!) Because ladies first!' and they both burst out laughing. He turns around and looks at her again, '*Aap Madhur ho, na?* (You're Madhur, right?) Maddie Vlogs from Goa?'

Her ears burn. How is it even possible that an actual Bollywood star—belonging to the yesteryears, yes—actually knows her!

'I've seen your videos, and I like them,' he tells her, as they walk down the steps, aware of everyone's gaze on them. Madhur is tongue tied. He winks at her, snatches her phone from her hand and takes a selfie of them together. She quickly regains her composure and opens her mouth, 'Sir, *ék* Insta Reel *ho jaye?* (Sir, how about one Insta Reel?) Please? It will help my channel get more subscribers,' she pleads.

'Not here, *kahin aur chaléin* (can we go somewhere else)? Somewhere quiet. You have a car?' he asks. 'Scooter,' she says, suddenly embarrassed by it.

'Follow me then.'

What? Madhur can't believe that he actually agreed. He gets into his car and zooms off. She starts chasing his silver Porsche 718 Boxter through the lanes of Arradi. Obviously, she cannot keep up. He has to slow down every few minutes for her to catch up. Exasperated, he brakes and flags her down. She pulls over by his window and leans inside, to be able to hear him above the

noise of his revving engine. He knocks on her helmet, 'Go park your khatara at that bar—the owner's my friend—and hop into my car,' he shouts. She does as she is told and hesitantly slides into the front seat beside him. A million thoughts run amok inside her head. Remembering her mobile, she fumbles while taking it out of her pocket, and drops it on the car floor.

'No!' he says. 'Use my iPhone,' and hands it to her.

'But how will I—'

'Bluetooth *ya* WhatsApp *karoonga*!'

Madhur nods. Of course! How stupid of her …

'Start,' he orders. Madhur's brain is smashed to smithereens. 'Where are we going?' she asks, buying some time to retrieve the fragments. '*Batana padéga na* (Will have to tell) …'

'Chapora River Bank.'

'Okay, ready?' she asks. 'I won't go live—I'll edit the footage and then upload,' she tells him.

'Okay! Action!' he barks.

MADHUR: Oh my God! Friends, you won't believe what I'm doing right now! My hair is flying at 140 kms per hour … *aur main baithi hoon ék mashoor star ki car méin* (I am sitting in a superstar's car)!! OMG, friends, OMG!

Switching the camera mode, she frames the middle-aged superstar.

MADHUR: See who I'm with! Can you believe it? I JUST CANNOT!!! I am with Ricky Malhotra! And here we are, at the famous Chapora riverbank in Siolim.

She gets out and shoots Ricky Malhotra posing against his car, doing quick pans from the car, the star and the river. It's almost 12 noon and the blinding sun beats down on them.

The middle-aged superstar gestures 'cut' and returns to his car. '*Phir karéngé* (Will do it again), another day, morning or evening time,' he says to her. 'Too bright, the sun will cast deep shadows on my face.' Madhur nods in agreement and stops filming. 'Get in, I'll drop you to your scooter,' he says.

Madhur is elated with the promise of a future second shoot. How fortuitous that she should bump into such a famous personality on a routine errand. But this is Goa, and the strangest things are known to happen here. Superstars, who normally avoid fans in big cities, converse with them like old friends over here. Perhaps it's a mutual recognition of their love for Goa. For Madhur, Ricky Malhotra comes across as down-to-earth, and the importance and respect he accords her is the biggest revelation. All those rumours she had heard about him in popular media are totally misguided, she tells herself as she leans back into his plush car seat, marvelling at the world outside blurring past at an insane speed. This is the fastest car she has ever sat in. When Ricky casually puts his arm around her shoulder, she doesn't mind—in fact, she smiles at him.

'Okay if I stop and smoke?' he asks her, slowing down suddenly. They are in an isolated stretch, with no human habitation in sight. 'This is a quiet spot, *itminaan sé smoke karoonga* (will smoke at ease)!' he says. 'You know, Madhur, we Bollywood stars have to be very careful nowadays. *Yeh media walley toh hummé smoke bhi karney nahi détéy! Chup-chup ké karna padta hain sab kucch!* (These media people won't even let us smoke! We have to do everything in hiding!)'

'I understand,' she says. 'Mind if I bum a cigarette?' she asks, trying to sound blasé.

'*Bhidu, main* cigarette *nahin phoonkta!* (Buddy, I don't smoke cigarettes!)' he says, lighting a doobie and taking a drag, before passing it to her. Madhur takes a long puff and smiles, 'I've smoked more kadak ganja than this,' she says.

'*Accha?* You prefer something more kadak? *Teri toh!* (I'll show you!)' he guffaws and ruffles her hair.

Madhur smiles at Ricky as he continues playing with her hair whilst looking straight ahead and smoking. Suddenly, he grabs her hair and pulls her from her seat. Using one leg, he positions her in the tight space between his legs and the car controls. Opening his zipper, he pushes down her head with one hand, smoking nonchalantly with the other. After some time, his grip on her head slackens, and she quickly slides back to her seat and wipes her lips with the cuff of her sleeve.

Ricky Malhotra starts the car and drives as if nothing happened. He glances sideways at Madhur and notices a drop of semen at the corner of her lips. He wipes it away gently with his thumb and turns his attention back to the road. They arrive at the bar where her scooter is parked. Madhur opens the car door and walks away without looking back. 'Wait', he says, 'take your phone,' and chucks it at her. She looks at her phone and notices that along with the videos and photos she took with his iPhone, he has also sent her his number and a map to his Goa villa.

'Call me,' he says. '*Proper shoot karengey*. (Will shoot a proper video.)'

Madhur rides fast and reaches Casa Coutinho. She runs straight to her bathroom, opens a Listerine bottle and gargles vigorously. She washes her mouth over and over till the bottle is half.

'Once is enough dear,' says Mrs Coutinho, 'quite expensive it is.'

Madhur smiles weakly and steps outside, giving Mrs Coutinho the house tax receipt from her pocket.

'Hope you didn't make videos in the Panchayat?'

'No, Auntyji.'

'Then you went somewhere else to shoot? Why so sunburnt?' Mrs Coutinho asks. Madhur fidgets uncomfortably and does not answer. Mrs Coutinho realizes she is intruding and softens her tone, 'Come for lunch then, I've made your favourite prawn curry.'

'I'm not hungry, Auntyji. I'll take a nap, not feeling well.'

'Hope you wore your mask? All kinds of people come to the Panchayat.'

Absolutely, thinks Madhur.

CHAPTER 8

Video Killed the Radio Star

Madhur edits her videos of the 1980s' superstar at night. She deletes the last dialogue and adds a voice over asking people to visit Goa. '*Yahan kuch bhi ho sakta hain!* (Anything can happen here!)' she says, signing off. She tags Goa Tourism, several travel agencies, airlines and hotel chains while uploading it as a late video. That done, she shuts her laptop and takes her mobile to bed. Her neck feels stiff and the soles of her feet hurt. She attributes it to her morning escapade, riding hard on her 'khatara' to keep pace with a bloody Porsche ...

Enraged, she flicks on her mobile camera and starts filming in selfie mode in the dark.

'*Saala maadarchod* (Bloody motherfucker), Ricky Malhotra! Who does he think he is? Bloody shit, two seconds *bhi nahi tik paaya* (couldn't stay up) ...'

She laughs as tears roll down her face. The camera has adjusted its settings to compensate for low light; her video looks like Madhur Witch Project. She deletes it and wipes her tears. It's been a rather tiring day, with the incident leaving a bad taste in her mouth. No amount of toothpaste or mouthwash seems to help. Even Mrs Coutinho's prawn curry tasted odd at dinner.

She tosses and turns through the night, exasperated that she feels an urge to pee every half hour. Surfing through YouTube, she looks at other blogger's videos on Goa, making a note of what not to do. Next, she looks at video-editing tutorials, before finally falling asleep at dawn.

Mrs Coutinho's voice sounds far-away, as if she's calling out from a distant room. Madhur opens her eyes. 'Don't want to get up?' Mrs Coutinho asks her, 'It's almost lunch time.' Madhur looks at her mobile—it was continuously pinging through the morning, but she was too tired to check. There are four-digit notifications on her social media icons. She doesn't know what to check first. Scores of people have commented on her video. As she reads the comments one by one, the screen starts to blur and her eyes hurt. Dragging herself out of bed, she goes to the bathroom. A cold bath energizes her—but only for a minute. She feels drained as she walks slowly to the dining room for lunch.

'You look pale, my child,' Mrs Coutinho says, bringing her palm close to Madhur's forehead to check for fever. Madhur screams 'Stop!' and cowers, as if the old lady was brandishing a red-hot iron. Startled at her extreme reaction, Mrs Coutinho asks, 'What happened?' Madhur looks crestfallen as she whispers the word 'COVID-19.'

'Hehh! Just a fever,' Mrs Coutinho laughs, 'Because you were dancing in the afternoon sun with Superstar Ricky Malhotra! I know! My daughter Stella saw your video and told me. Big fans of Malhotra we both are, haan …'

'No, Mrs Coutinho, it feels like more than a fever,' she says. 'NO, NO, don't touch.' Madhur runs inside her room and locks the door. 'I'll stay inside here. Don't come near me and don't tell anybody.'

Mrs Coutinho says a quick prayer at the altar. Then, she goes to Madhur's closed door and blesses her from outside. 'It's all my fault. Why did I send you to the Panchayat? There was so much crowd because of that bloody Malhotra bugger ... Forgive me O lord,' she says.

'Forgive me, O Bhagwan,' Madhur whispers fervently, falling to her knees on the other side of the door. 'I shouldn't have swallowed ...'

Mrs Coutinho quickly consults her family doctor over the phone. 'Don't take her to any hospital or government clinic,' he says. 'Just give her paracetamol, some chicken soup and observe from a safe distance. Young people fight the infection in three to four days,' he tells her. 'I'll drop by with the medicine, and listen, Mabel ... don't tell neighbours or family,' he advises Mrs Coutinho.

Madhur sleeps through the next five days, leaving the bed only to relieve herself and swallow bowls of soup and a tasteless watery gruel that Mrs Coutinho keeps on the threshold of her room. Her body aches like she was hit by a Porsche, the pain radiating from outside in. Every toss and turn on the bed hurts. Forget shooting videos, she can't even look at her mobile screen. For the first time since she started using a mobile—at twelve—and since she had a smart phone with social media apps—at fourteen—Madhur has left hers unattended for five days.

On the sixth day of quarantining, Madhur is concerned when Mrs Coutinho enters her room suddenly—she has already served the morning soup and there are still three hours left for lunch. She stands at the threshold looking disturbed, searching for the right words to speak.

'That actor bugger—he died, today morning,' Mrs Coutinho says finally.

'Who?' Madhur sits up.

'Your Malhotraji ... God knows how. News channels reported that his diabetes became very high and then his heart stopped. I thought I should tell you.'

'So, it wasn't COVID-19,' Madhur says, feeling relieved.

'There's a debate on TV, and some doctor is saying that COVID-19 medicines make diabetes shoot up,' Mrs Coutinho explains. 'Ricky Malhotra's wife is shouting that someone from the panchayat gave it to him—she's blaming the sarpanch. The whole panchayat and whoever was present that day, have been asked to quarantine.'

'I'm already doing it,' Madhur smiles.

'Have you told anyone that you're sick? Put any videos on internet?'

'No, Auntyji, my phone's dead—I haven't charged it for a week.'

'If people get to know you're sick, they'll say you gave him the COVID-19 virus. Then all those reporters will come here and shout at you. And me also.' Mrs Coutinho starts hyperventilating.

'Relax, Auntyji. I think he gave it to me!'

Madhur gets up and searches for her mobile charger. Plugging her phone for charging, she goes for a bath after six days of no bathing. The scalding hot water makes her lightheaded, she steps out of the bathroom and flops on her bed for a bit. Her phone rings, startling her—she's forgotten her own ringtone! It's an unknown number; she hesitates at first, but picks it up.

'Is that Maddie Vlogs?' asks a sweet voice.

'Haanji, Madhur Chopra speaking, "Maddie Vlogs from Goa", who are you?'

'I'm Ramona Malhotra,' says the lady, with a clipped, fancy accent.

Madhur's stomach turns. It's the last person she wants to speak to right now.

'Hello, you there?'

'Haanji,' Madhur responds.

'I'd like to meet you,' Ramona says.

'I'm in Delhi,' says Madhur, 'On work. I'll be back after two weeks—maybe three. Can I meet you then?'

'Oh, aren't you sick?'

'*Bilkul nahin ji* (Absolutely not), I'm toh absolutely fine. Sorry about Malhotraji, *Bhagwaan unki aatma ko shanti dé* (May God bless his soul),' Madhur says, her heart beating at 140 kmph.

'You're lying!' Ramona says sharply. 'Why was your mobile switched off for so many days? Were you in hospital?'

Madhur is shitting bricks now. 'O nahin ji, I have two mobiles—one for working, one for vlogging. When I'm working, I switch off my vlogging mobile … distraction hota hain na …'

'Okay,' Ramona says and ends the call.

Madhur heaves a huge sigh of relief at having dodged a bullet.

Part II

PART II

CHAPTER 9

Between a Dank and a Dark Place

The video Madhur had posted of superstar Ricky Malhotra has gone viral as his last appearance on camera. Several TV channels air it without her permission. Shradanjali shows broadcast her footage of the superstar posing against his car by the river. 'What a great place to die! In Goa, one is already in heaven!' is repeated by every news channel, plastering Madhur's and Ricky's face side by side on their screens. Her vlog names are constantly repeated by anchors.

Random people start checking out her social feeds, leaving tasteless comments on her posts. They have no interest in her outfits, no understanding of high fashion, or her photography; they just want to troll. Many want to meet her and take a selfie with her, to flex on their own feeds. For the first time, Madhur is scared of her increasing subscriber and follower base. She deactivates all her social media accounts temporarily, locking herself inside her room, drawing all the curtains and not stepping outside the villa. It's a good thing that some old Goan houses are so cavernous, one can easily hole up inside and go undetected for years. 'Why are you hiding?' Mrs Coutinho asks.

'It's not your fault. How many days will you stay inside? You've already spent six days doing quarantine.'

'I don't know, Auntyji. I may have to quarantine for 100 years ...'

'Hehh! Mad or what!'

The vaddo neighbours keep news reporters at bay, telling them that Madhur has not been seen for days. 'Must've have gone back to North—she was from there only, no? Delhi? No UP, bhaiyya-girl, I think. God knows men, she went back I think—good only it is!'

With all access to Madhur gone, her older, loyal followers start worrying about her. They send her emails begging her to reactivate her accounts, but Madhur is not checking her emails either. Rumours are rife on social media.

'Has Maddie died, just like Ricky Malhotra? Have Maddie and Malhotra walked into the COVID-19 sunset, hand-in-hand?'

Madhur is unaware of all this prattling going on behind her back, on the internet.

'At least get up and walk in the garden,' Mrs Coutinho beseeches her one morning. Madhur has had breakfast and promptly hit the bed again. 'Don't sleep all day, your body will get heavy,' Mrs Coutinho says, looking worried.

'I'm feeling strange, Auntyji—actually, I don't feel at all. Is that possible?'

'Don't talk rubbish! C'mon, get up now. It's so beautiful outside. It's 9.00 a.m. and there's mist in the coconut grove,' saying this, she goes back to her kitchen duties.

Madhur sits up, and out of habit pats the bed, searching for her mobile. On finding it, she doesn't know what to do with it. It's been switched off for weeks now. She walks past Mrs Coutinho in the kitchen, and out the back door into the backyard.

'Take photo of the flowers,' Mrs Coutinho urges her. Madhur smiles apologetically, she isn't carrying her mobile.

It is indeed a lovely October morning. As she walks in the dew drenched grass, a beautiful bird song catches her ears. She surveys the backyard, looking for the bird. In her five months of living with Mrs Coutinho, this is the first time she has ventured out here.

The sunshine filtering through coconut fronds, paints her body in stripes. Definitely not the look of this season, she concurs. A narrow plume of smoke gently wafts above the outdoor bathroom, from bathwater kept on firewood for heating. The smell of burning firewood reminds Madhur of the *chullah* (clay oven) that Ramnarayanji—the old chowkidar at her college campus, used for making his rotis. He had a gas stove in his little *kothi* (cabin), but preferred to cook on an improvised chullah. '*Gas ka khana shahri lagta hain ji, chull'hé ka khana ghar jaisa lagta hain!* (Food cooked on gas tastes very city-like, but food cooked on a clay oven tastes home-cooked!)' he'd say.

Madhur sighs and sits down on her haunches, leaning against a coconut tree. During her college days, she had spent many similar moments in the Delhi Development Area (DDA) park close to home, accompanied by a cigarette—which she smoked sneakily, lest someone familiar spotted her and tattled to her father. She shat out all her project ideas in this position—on her haunches with a cigarette in hand. Her rich classmates probably did the same, but on their fancy Kohler commodes.

Besides, their parents allowed them to smoke at home—can you believe that!

Madhur pretend-smokes and, for the sake of authenticity, takes a long drag, holding two fingers up. She cannot understand what she is feeling. Is it freedom? Having snapped all the digital umbilical cords that bound her to the outside world, she feels lighter, almost transcendent. She has no desire for anything beyond the boundaries of her body and her mind. Wait, is this how madness begins?

After three empty puffs, she decides she would rather smoke a beedi and changes the positioning of her fingers. Shaking her head she smiles wryly, no ideas are coming to her this time. Her mind is blank.

She sees a bright red bug, about a centimetre long, with a black diamond shape on its back, flitting about in the soil. It happily climbs over her slipper-clad feet in its quest to get at the coconut tree roots. She is surprised that she does not flinch, but the bug isn't ticklish either. Now a big black ant wanders over her foot, '*Behenchod saali! Kaat gayi!* (Fucking bitch! She bit me),' Madhur screams, and has to pry away the offending critter with her fingers. Just then Mrs Coutinho calls out from the backdoor, 'Madhur, come quick, your mummy is on the phone!'

With great effort, she gets up and walks inside the house. She picks up the receiver of the rotary dial phone in Mrs Coutinhos' sala. '*Bétaa,* mobile *kyun* switched off *hain? Kitna try kiya! Maar daalégi tu mujhé* (Child, why is your mobile switched off? I tried calling you! You'll kill me one day),' her mother sobs dramatically.

'Sorry, Mummyji,' Madhur replies, 'I don't know *kya ho raha hai* (what is happening) ... I feel ... numb. *Kya main mar chuki hoon?* (Am I dead?)'

Mrs Coutinho grabs the receiver from Madhur's hand and says, 'Don't worry, Damayanti dear, I'll take care of your daughter. She's just tired right now, that's why she's not making sense. But *main hoon na* (I am here) ...'

'Thank you ji, thank you ji, *aapka ehsaan hain mujhpé* (I am indebted to you),' Mrs Damayanti Devi Chopra says.

'Okay, okay,' Mrs Coutinho says and disconnects. She looks at Madhur and sighs deeply. 'What's the matter, child?'

Madhur does not meet Mrs Coutinho's gaze, she is looking down at her feet. The area where the ant bit her is now swollen to a red bump, and it is burning like scalding hot water has been poured on it. Mrs Coutinho lifts up Madhur's face by cupping her hand around her chin, 'Talk to me, dear. Tell me what's going on. Should I call my doctor? He'll give you some tonic, and you'll be fine in two days.'

'Okay, Auntyji.'

Mrs Coutinho is perturbed. Madhur is behaving just like her neighbour Maria's daughter, Anna, had behaved when her husband eloped with a foreigner lady. 'Madhur, dear, has a boy said something to you?' she asks hesitantly, 'or, done something?'

Madhur's face crumbles, and she points to her feet, 'No, Auntyji, an ant bit me.' She starts bawling.

Mrs Coutinho sits down at Madhur's feet and closely examines the swelling, 'Just checking if it's something else,' Mrs Coutinho says, hoping it's not a snake bite. There are rat snakes and cobras roaming freely in the coconut grove, but they rarely bother humans, being more afraid of us, than we could be of them. 'No, ant bite only. I'll put ice on it, okay?' she says relieved, and goes towards the refrigerator.

'I'll do it, Auntyji,' Madhur says, regaining her composure and running ahead.

Mrs Coutinho cannot erase the sight of Madhur crying over an ant bite. Should she tell Stella—who's also concerned at not seeing any new videos from "Maddie Vlogs in Goa"? After the initial irritation, Stella has slowly warmed up to Madhur. She now proudly shows off Madhur's videos of Goa and her house to her friends and neighbours in the UK.

'COVID-19 depression,' declares Stella.

'Shush! Don't say that!'

'It's been proven,' Stella insists vehemently. 'People here are suffering the same. Long COVID-19 causes it. The NHS says it can last for a year.'

'Shut up! Anything you talk!' Mrs Coutinho scolds her daughter. 'All this nonsense happens to white people only,' she says. 'Doctor Fernandes will just look at her and make her alright.'

CHAPTER 10

Not Feni

Dr Fernandes concurs that Madhur has a case of low-functioning depression, after a two-hour-long chat with her. He tells Mrs Coutinho, 'She's gone through a lot—her dad's untimely death due to COVID-19, work disruptions, having to find new ways to make money. You know, Mabel, these youngsters had taken their world for granted, and now it has crumbled in front of their eyes. I'm called every day to counsel so many, even six-year-olds are depressed! I don't know what's happening, Mabel. This COVID-19 and all is on one side, but there's something else ... Are we responsible for this? Did we stop connecting with our children?' Dr Fernandes muses.

'I don't know all that—will Madhur get better?' Mrs Coutinho asks.

'Give her time, she'll be fine.'

'And medicines? Give her some pills and tonic, no?'

'Not required. Just keep a watch on her,' Dr Fernandes says, 'and give her work—lots of it! Make her help you with housework, send her out on errands, let her work in the garden—being out in nature is the best cure for depression.

Madhur needs structure in her life. Constantly living online on digital devices is bad for mental health,' he says, waving goodbye.

Mrs Coutinho waves back and shuts the main gate. She goes to the backyard and picks up a bucket of washed clothes—her maid had left in a rush today, without putting them out to dry. She walks slowly with the heavy bucket and starts pinning them on a clothesline tied between two mango trees. She is worried about the doctor's prognosis. It reminds her of what had happened to Anna. After three months of moping around and doing nothing, Anna, a young mother of two boys, suddenly picked herself up and started singing at night clubs. 'How else will I feed my boys? And who'll pay their school fees? I have to do something, no?' Anna told her mother, Maria. But soon, Anna started wearing small dresses, exactly like the foreigner lady her husband had eloped with.

Mrs Coutinho holds one of Madhur's short skirts and shakes out the creases, 'But Madhur already wears short skirts' she mutters. Then again, Mrs Coutinho remembers, after one month of singing in nightclubs, Anna started smoking weird looking cigarettes. All her clothes reeked of a weird smell—definitely not tobacco. Mrs Coutinho quickly hangs the rest of the clothes and rushes to Madhur's room. Her heart skips a beat seeing Madhur dressed in a full-sleeved hoodie and full length harem pants. She's lying on her bed, reading a book from Godfrey's library. Mrs Coutinho quickly starts dusting the furniture.

'Oh Auntyji, *aap chodd do, main karti hoon* (leave it, I'll do it)!' Madhur says, jumping up from her bed, looking embarrassed. 'My room is my responsibility, Auntyji. I dusted yesterday, see! It's clean.'

'You are still recovering, my child ... so I thought, I'll clean,' she says, looking around as if searching for dust balls. Or weird cigarettes. Satisfied at not finding any, she leaves Madhur to her book.

'She is reading Daddy's books,' Mrs Coutinho whispers to Stella over the receiver. It's 6.00 p.m., the customary mother-daughter phone call time.

'She wants to become a lawyer?' Stella enquires.

'No, no, not those books. She is reading the fat novels—Hemingroad, Stainbox and ... Romeo-Juliet fellow.'

'Mom! It's Hemingway, Steinbeck and Shakespeare!'

Mrs Coutinho harrumphs and says, 'You understood, no?'

'That's a good thing, Mumma. Those books changed my life. Look where I am.'

'Chehh! Her parents don't want her to become an English teacher,' Mrs Coutinho says dismissively. 'I'm worried because she's doing things she never did before.'

'It's all good, Mumma, relax! I gotta sleep now, goodnight.'

'*Déo borém korum, déo borim raat dium!* (May God bless you with a good night!),' Mrs Coutinho blesses her daughter and disconnects the call.

Mrs Coutinho says the angelus prayer at 7.00 p.m. and goes to the kitchen to supervize the dinner that the maid is preparing. Madhur joins them at the long kitchen platform to cut vegetables for a salad. Ten people can easily stand side by side and work at the platform. 'You know, my Godfrey had four sisters and three brothers—all older than him. I don't know how my mother-in-law managed so many children, cooking for them, cleaning for them—they had lots of servants of course. So much food she must've cooked—you see those big utensils in the corner—she used them every day!' Mrs Coutinho says, pointing to a stack of massive copper utensils, blackened with dust and non-use. 'Now these small steel ones are enough for us,' she says to Madhur.

'So where are Uncle Godfrey's brothers and sisters? Do they also live in Goa?'

'No, they all went to Portugal when Goa became a part of India—only my Godfrey stayed behind, to look after his old parents. His siblings have all passed away, and their children are much older than Stella.'

'Don't they come to Goa? Your nephews and nieces …'

'No, they've all become full Portuguese now and cannot manage in Goa—but forget them! Their mothers or their fathers are Portuguese, so they're only half Goan—but my Stella behaves like she's full English. More English than the bloody queen, men!'

'Auntyji, why do so many Goans go to the UK and other foreign countries? They leave their big-big houses and go live in those bloody cold countries … why? *Goa mein kya kami hain?* (What is lacking in Goa?)'

'Not enough work opportunities here, my dear,' Mrs Coutinho explains. 'And we, older Goans, still have our Portuguese passports. So, our children and grandchildren can easily become Portuguese citizens and migrate to the UK and EU countries. More money and work opportunities there. Even sweepers there make more money than bank managers in Goa, I'm told.'

Madhur and Mrs Coutinho carry the serving bowls to the dinner table. Mrs Coutinho likes to set the large table—which seats twelve people—with table mats, napkins and cutlery. She always places fresh flowers from the garden in a big round crystal vase at the centre. Two tall, burnished metal candlestands with lit candles are kept on both sides of the flower arrangement. The maid serves them dinner, washes utensils, packs leftovers for her family and leaves Casa Coutinho by 9.00 p.m.

When Madhur had dinner for the first time with Mrs Coutinho, she thought the old woman was showing off her Portuguese ancestry. Madhur was uncomfortable throughout the dinner service, afraid that she would drop something and unsure about which spoons and forks to use. She was afraid of dropping tomato soup on the delicate lace table mats. She didn't know whether to cut the bread with a fork or a knife—or to cut it at all. She was so tense that she did not enjoy her meal and felt relieved when dinner was over. But to her consternation, it continued every night.

Madhur preferred eating on the run, so she could get back to editing her videos or blogging about her day. Mrs Coutinho's theatrical dinner service, amusing at first, became a spot of bother and Madhur had to cook up new excuses every night to avoid eating at the table. Poor Mrs Coutinho cut a lonely figure at the massive table, sighing deeply and eating alone.

After dinner, Madhur joins Mrs Coutinho in the sala with a bottle of feni and a chilled coke. 'Here you go,' she says, giving a 60ml shot to the old woman, who prefers it neat and sips it slowly for an hour. For herself, Madhur pours a tiny 15ml peg and tops it up with chilled coke. This is their new routine every night at 10.00 p.m., ever since she recovered from COVID-19. 'Have it neat,' Mrs Coutinho reprimands her. 'That soft drink will make your feni useless!'

'Auntyji, I cannot! I'm used to beer, whisky or vodka. It'll take time to appreciate this taste.'

'See! That's the problem! You're drinking it like whisky-vodka-beer. We Goans drink it like medicine—and it is! Why do you think I didn't get COVID-19 from you? Because of this,' Mrs Coutinho says, crinkling her nose and inhaling the aroma from her glass.

CHAPTER 11

Fairy Godfather

It's 5.30 a.m. and pitch dark outside; Madhur is up earlier than usual. Mrs Coutinho is already puttering about in the kitchen. Madhur enters the kitchen and greets her. 'Get four poes and five pãos today. I'm making chicken xacuti for lunch,' Mrs Coutinho says, handing the bread bag to Madhur.

'Oh wow! Then I won't eat breakfast, Auntyji!'

'How you'll not eat? Of course, you will. After walking so much, you'll eat me also,' Mrs Coutinho laughs. Madhur rolls her eyes and leaves.

Every morning she walks 3 kilometres to the village bakery, in spite of its doorstep delivery service. She's been advised to take morning walks by Dr Fernandes. Previously, Madhur would step out this early only if she had to shoot videos or take pictures, but now she's happy to be of assistance to Mrs Coutinho.

Madhur buys the bread and starts walking back, alternating between a slow jog and a fast walk down the Parra-Assagão Road. Near the Assagão junction, a middle-aged gentleman jogging past, stops and says hello. Madhur is now accustomed to strangers smiling and waving at her—she's a Parra celebrity.

She mostly feels uncomfortable with the attention. Any conversation with these fans invariably leads to them asking her why she isn't vlogging or posting on her social media accounts anymore. To that, Madhur has no answer. So, she does the customary slow wave and puts her head down.

The middle-aged gentleman continues walking beside her, even after the initial acknowledgement nods are exchanged. Thankfully, Madhur no longer panics when something like this happens; the post-traumatic stress disorder (PTSD) induced by Delhi streets is now a distant memory.

'I'm Karl Mascarenhas, Mrs Coutinho's nephew. You were supposed to call me,' he says. 'Oh! Auntyji told me, but I forgot. I'm so sorry.'

'No problem, Madhur, but I need your help urgently,' he says. 'My event is on 31 October, and only four days are left.'

'Karlji, I don't vlog anymore.'

'Just call me Karl, no "ji"!' he says and smiles. 'Madhur, I need a stage design, no vlogging or influencing.'

'Oh … it's been a long time since I did any set or stage design,' she hesitates.

'I'll pay ₹10,000,' Karl says. 'And a couple more, if you help with organizing—we always need extra hands on the show day.' He waits for her to respond. That amount is Madhur's one month's rent. She has been dipping into her savings for the past two months. 'What's your event concept?' she asks.

'I'm going to the venue—come along, I'll explain.'

Madhur hesitates, 'I've to drop this home,' she says, showing him the bread bag. 'Coutinho Auntyji will be waiting,' she says. 'Can I join you later?'

'We'll pass Casa Coutinho on the way—the venue's close to it.' Karl explains.

They jog side by side and cover the remaining distance to Casa Coutinho. Karl follows Madhur inside and greets his aunt cheerily. While aunt and nephew are exchanging pleasantries, Madhur goes to her room and changes out of her sweaty exercise clothes. Karl and Madhur walk to the venue—a large wedding garden-type place, off the Parra-Saligão Road.

One set of labourers is busy polishing a wooden stage and another set is clearing the overgrown garden area. A metal truss to hold light fittings is being erected by technicians. 'I'm organising a Halloween Night,' Karl tells her. 'For almost a year all events in Goa were cancelled, but my show will be the first big show. I want something totally different.'

'Haan, something out-of-the-box, na?' Madhur asks sarcastically.

'No, out-of-the-pumpkin,' Karl says and guffaws.

'Is Halloween celebrated by Goans?' she asks.

'Not really, it's an American thing. We celebrate All Souls Day on 2 November, two days later—that's big with us Goan Catholics. But clubs and restaurants organize Halloween-themed parties for youngsters like you,' Karl explains.

'Oh! So, Diwali this year is on the same day as All Souls Day!' Madhur exclaims.

'Ya, it's a bit odd this year—I mean, Diwali is the festival of lights, a celebration of life, while All Souls Day is a celebration of death. In fact, in Mexico, it's called the "Day of the Dead"—*Día de Muertos*,' explains Karl.

'Really? What happens on this day?'

'Don't know about the Mexican tradition—I'm told they have elaborate rituals. But in Goa, we go to the cemetery and clean up all the overgrown grass around the graves of our relatives, place fresh flowers and pray for their souls,' Karl explains.

'Accha! That's why "All Souls Day".'

'It's great for us, if the two festivals are on the same day—we'll get a bigger crowd, more people will be in Goa. We'll follow all COVID-19 protocols though—masks and hand sanitizers.'

'Chalo, I'll go home and start designing. Please can you drop me back to Casa Coutinho? I already had enough of walking for today.'

'Sure,' he says, and goes to his parked car. 'But before that, I'll treat you to something interesting—actually, I want to eat it and you are my excuse! Jacinta, my wife, gets mad when I eat breakfast outside,' he says, as Madhur sits in his car. 'Even Coutinho Auntyji will get mad at me,' she says. 'What are we going to eat?'

'The best Ros omelette in Goa.'

'Oh no, no,' Madhur says, as Karl drives down the Parra-Saligão Road, in the opposite direction of Casa Coutinho. It's 9.30 a.m., and they arrive just in time to be served the last order. Madhur quickly dons her sunglasses and her mask. As Karl chats animatedly in Konkani with the gaado guy, Madhur falls back slowly, trying to put sufficient distance between the cart and herself. Karl turns to her and says, 'Maddie, this is my school friend, Peter.' Turning to Peter he says, 'She's a famous designer from Delhi, she's doing my event design.'

'Oh, very good, very good. She's doing real work,' Peter says, not taking his eyes off the skillet. Madhur detects a hint of sarcasm in his tone and wants the earth to swallow her. She takes her plate of Ros omelette and walks away from the cart, stands at a distance with her back to Karl and Peter, lowers her mask, and starts eating it. Karl joins her, wondering why she's eating so furtively. 'Not used to eating on the road?' he enquires.

'I prefer sitting at a table,' she lies.

'Aye, Peter! You must put some tables and chairs here, men!'

'For what? People will not leave only! They'll sit here, play cards—or they'll put plates on the table and take pictures … naka re! This is only good. With a plate in their hands, they have to eat and leave.'

CHAPTER 12

Demons at Mapusa Bus Stand

Madhur does not attend Karl's Halloween event or help with organizing it, pulling out at the last minute.

A day earlier, while listening to the bands practising, she had covered her ears and said to Karl, 'I don't like this engineering college-type music. I prefer Kay Kay, Shaan, Prateep Kuhad, Arijit Singh …'

'Oh, you like Bollywood music.' Karl looked disappointed, but did not force her. '*Theek hain* here are your design fees,' he said, giving her a cheque and disappearing back inside the venue.

The Halloween event is a big success—as he'd predicted—getting featured in all local newspapers, with his smiling face splashed in the entertainment sections. Mrs Coutinho though, is quite upset the next morning. She has two papers spread open on the dining table. 'Even your picture would have come here, why didn't you go last night?' she asks Madhur. 'I would have called Stella and said, "See! Madhur's photo comes in newspapers …"'

'Arré, Auntyji, I don't listen to Rock-shock.'

'Oh, so you think it's the devil's music!' Mrs Coutinho laughs. 'Who's the old lady now?'

'Auntyji! I'm ancient, you are toh sweet sixteen,' Madhur says. She has Diwali on her mind and she's not sure if she can celebrate it in a Catholic household. 'Auntyji', she asks hesitantly, 'would it be okay if I light Diwali diyas in my balcony and window?'

'Of course! I thought you don't like bursting crackers, putting lights … Go buy from Mapusa market.'

'Yes, yes, Auntyji. I'll go now.'

'And by the way, are you going to see the Narkasurs tonight? Or will you sit at home again?'

'*Woh kya hain?* (What is that?)'

'You don't know? Don't they have that in Delhi? It's celebrated before Diwali? People light those big things on fire, afterwards …'

'Oh, you mean Ram-Leela?' Madhur asks. 'But that's earlier, at Dussehra.'

'Not Ram-Leela, Narkasur!' Mrs Coutinho corrects her. 'You don't go out these days, or you would've seen them everywhere.'

'Seen whom, Auntyji?'

'See, it's like this. Groups of Hindu boys make Paper maché effigies of a demon called Narkasur. They fill him with crackers. On Diwali morning, they burn him. But before that, there is a competition. The best Narkasurs win prizes.'

'What! Where can I see them?' Madhur asks, laughing.

'Mapusa bus stand has a Narkasur parade. Panjim also,' Mrs Coutinho tells her. 'But you don't go alone—too much crowd. There will be hooligans. Go with Karl; he takes Jacinta every year.' Saying this, Mrs Coutinho immediately calls Karl. She tells him something in Konkani in a lowered voice, ends the call, and smiles at Madhur. 'He said yes. Be ready by 11.00 p.m. tonight, he'll pick you up.'

'But Auntyji, I sleep at that time. It'll be too late,' Madhur protests. She has just got acquainted professionally with Karl, and it doesn't seem appropriate to socialize with him and his wife. But Mrs Coutinho insists, 'When you're my age, you sleep at 11,' she says sternly. 'Why you came to Goa? Should've stayed in Delhi only, where girls can't step out at night. Go out and enjoy, be with friends, meet new people ... don't sit home all day and night. No wonder doctor says you have depresshun.'

Madhur feels suitably chastened by Mrs Coutinho's tirade. 'Okay! I'll go,' she says to her, 'but only if you come along.'

Karl arrives at midnight to pick them up. Madhur has fallen asleep on a sofa in the sala—all dressed and ready to go since 10.00 p.m. Mrs Coutinho wakes her up and offers to make coffee for Karl, Jacinta and a groggy Madhur. Everybody refuses and they rush to his car. Karl apologizes for being late, introduces Jacinta to Madhur and drives maniacally to make it in time for the parade. They arrive at the Mapusa Bus Stand to the sound of crackers bursting. 'He didn't want to go, so tired he was from last night's Halloween show,' Jacinta says, looking adoringly at Karl. 'But when Aunty Mabel called saying Madhur wants to see Narkasurs, so quickly he changed his mind,' she teases him. She turns to Madhur and Mrs Coutinho in the backseat, 'Madhur, this is your first time seeing a Narkasur parade, na?'

Madhur nods. 'You Goans keep so many of your festivals secret, ya!'

'Everybody's only interested in celebrating New Year in Goa,' Karl says.

'And the Carnival Parade,' Jacinta adds.

Mrs Coutinho is engrossed in observing the crowds outside the car window. 'I don't remember the last time I saw Mapusa at midnight,' she says, lost in thoughts. 'Oh yes, when Stella was in school! Godfrey would bundle us all into his Premier Padmini, and off we'd go for the parades—Narkasur, Carnival and Shigmo ... but after Stella joined college, she started going with her friends. And Godfrey was not interested in taking out the car just for the two of us.'

Driving past the parade into Khorlim, Karl finds a vacant spot to park his car. They walk back the 500m distance to the Mapusa Bus Stand, jostling through crowds. Along the way, they pass several smaller Narkasur effigies made by youngsters outside their society buildings. The kids seem to be enjoying their own little celebrations, away from the larger, politician- and corporate-funded display. But whether the Narkasur is big or small, the endeavour—Madhur observes—is to make him look as hideous as possible. At the parade however, she spots quite a few Narkasurs looking like Gods. Some like Indianized Marvel superheroes almost, with bulging Hulk-like muscles. So, who's sticking to the creative brief, she wonders, the kids or the adults?

Karl leads them to a traffic police outpost at the bus stand. A couple of inspectors recognize him and quickly escort them out of the crowds. Plastic chairs are arranged for them so that they can get a ringside view of the parade. Noticing that just a minuscule number of people are wearing masks, Madhur quickly dons hers, gesturing to Jacinta and Mrs Coutinho to do the same. Karl laughs at her, 'COVID-19 is over,' he says. 'It's burnt out, just like the Narkasurs will soon be.'

Madhur watches awestruck at slow-moving trucks decorated with lights, genda phool, and mango leaves; carrying massive, gaudily painted effigies of demons. They are followed by processions of choreographed dancers and drummers. Most trucks have sound systems and DJs positioned underneath their Narkasur—nearly all of whom stand with their feet apart. As if the Narkasur has given birth to the DJ or, likely, shat him out. Some effigies are almost 15 to 20 feet tall.

Loud music rends the air, a cacophony of beats playing all at once. One particular sound is heard distinctively above the din—the sound of cymbals clashing. Madhur finds this sound grating; it's like giant scissors constantly gnashing beside her ears. She loves the drumming though. Mrs Coutinho gestures something with her forefinger and points a Narkasur to Madhur.

'What, Auntyji?' Madhur does not understand what she wants.

'Photo, photo, take photo!' Mrs Coutinho shouts to be heard. Madhur smiles, wondering why people still make the gesture of fingers pressing the shutter button on a camera. She takes out her mobile, frames Mrs Coutinho against a nasty-looking Narkasur, 'Smile, Auntyji!' she says, and lightly touches her mobile screen.

'Not me, *ago bai*! Take photo of Narkasur,' Mrs Coutinho chides her. 'Put on Instagram. Make video for YouTube. Then, Stella will also see in UK.'

'Auntyji, I'm shooting only for you—you send it to Stella if you want. I don't post on social media anymore, I told you na?' Madhur reminds Mrs Coutinho, taking photos and short videos for the first time since Superstar Ricky Malhotra. That's one demon slayed, she hopes.

Madhur notices an orange glow illuminating the eastern night sky. She points it out to Mrs Coutinho, exclaiming, 'Look, it's morning already. How quickly the night passed!' Karl overhears and looks at his watch, then in the east direction, 'Hehh, it's only 2.15 a.m.! That must be a big Narkasur coming along with strobe lights and all,' he says, getting all excited.

The orange glow grows bigger and brighter as it inches closer, reflecting on windows of the Mapusa market buildings, till it is a blazing ball of light that engulfs everything around. Madhur is mesmerized, unable to blink or move, when suddenly Karl and Mrs Coutinho yank her away from her spot. Four burly constables literally lift the three women and direct them to run to the other side of the parking lot. Madhur is sucked into a vortex of panicked people, getting separated from Mrs Coutinho, Karl and Jacinta. She is constantly steered in directions not of her choice. Her mobile slips out of her hand. She immediately drops on all fours, searching for it blindly between scrambling feet. Karl spots her and lifts her up, saying, 'Leave it! Leave it!' Madhur runs with him, holding his hand tightly, stealing a quick glance at the parade behind.

The entire street is engulfed in flames, firecrackers and rockets bursting in all directions, as all Narkasurs burn in unison. Scores of people are holding mobiles, filming the inferno.

Fortunately, the Mapusa Fire Station is a stone's throw away, and the engines arrive immediately, with sirens blaring and the firemen begging mobile phone-wielding crowds to disperse. As effigies continue to smoulder, their flaming paper maché pieces fall on the wooden truck floors, moving closer and closer to fuel tanks. As if timed perfectly in an action movie, the tanks explode one after the other. Madhur counts ten blasts, accompanied by showers of molten debris, fire engine bells tolling, and screams of people, and wonders if this is how a Rohit Shetty film set looks. If only someone had warned her in advance—she would have at least slung her mobile phone on a lanyard. Actually, she wasn't planning on filming at all. Her mobile was safe in her sling bag, but Mrs Coutinho wanted to show videos to Stella …

'This Narkasur parade is something else!' She says to Mrs Coutinho, who is sitting on the pavement outside a public garden, holding her head and sweating profusely. 'It's nothing like Ram-Leela. In Delhi, we have Ram-Leela on open grounds and people stand at a safe distance. But you Goans are crazy, you do everything differently!' Karl facepalms, then points in the direction of the blaze and says, 'Maddie, that is a fire! It's a mistake! We don't burn Narkasurs here—we also burn them on open grounds or in fields. God knows what happened this year … the world has gone to shit after COVID-19,' he says.

Madhur's jaw drops, 'So you're telling me that this Narkasur parade, on this narrow Mapusa market street, with effigies packed with firecrackers, all made of flammable material, moving atop diesel trucks, surrounded by crowds drinking and smoking … is safe?'

Karl ponders for a few seconds, 'You're right, we're fucking idiots … but then, for so many decades, things have gone smoothly.'

'More crowds this year,' Jacinta observes. 'Tourists have increased ten-fold.'

Turning to Mrs Coutinho, Karl says, 'Let's go home, Aunty Mabel.'

Mrs Coutinho mutters, as if speaking to herself, 'Didn't anybody see the fire?'

'I saw and showed you first,' says Madhur, as they trek slowly to Karl's car. All around them, people with burn wounds and bleeding bruises stagger like zombies, trying to escape the horror, or looking for medical attention. Ambulances arriving on the scene in droves immediately tend to the injured. 'And I didn't want to take pictures … because I'm a *panouti* (jinx), my mobile phone is a *panouti*, my social media accounts are a *panouti* …'

Jacinta puts an arm around Madhur, 'Don't be silly, girl. How could you have caused all this? This fire, it was just waiting to happen.'

They get into the car and Mrs Coutinho says a quick prayer to thank the lord for keeping them safe. She cries as she prays for people who were consumed by the fire. 'The Narkasurs are not demons,' she says. 'We are! Just look at us! Stuck to our phones, watching as if everything is a movie. It's happening right in front of our eyes and, yet, we'll see it through our phones.'

Karl and Jacinta wince, they put away their mobiles and stare at the road ahead. Madhur looks out the window, grateful to have lost hers.

CHAPTER 13

Let Us Rest in Pieces

It's 3.00 a.m. when they are dropped home. Madhur takes the keys from Mrs Coutinho and opens the main door. The old woman appears listless, as she continues to stand on the balcão. 'Come, Auntyji,' says Madhur, gently guiding her inside. She takes her to her room and assists her to her bed. Mrs Coutinho sits clutching the edge of her mattress, and stares at Madhur—not with gratitude, but with resignation. 'I'll take off your shoes—if you don't mind, Auntyji,' Madhur says and bends down, wondering if she should also help her change clothes. She decides not to; Mrs Coutinho is a proud, self-reliant lady. 'You rest now, change clothes tomorrow morning—arré, it's already morning!'

Mrs Coutinho points to the toilet. Madhur takes her to it and waits outside. Ten minutes later, Mrs Coutinho is still inside. There's absolute silence. Madhur waits for the flush sound. Another five minutes pass. She knocks on the slightly open door. 'Auntyji? All okay? You need help?'

'Help,' Mrs Coutinho says softly.

'I'm coming in,' says Madhur.

'In,' Mrs Coutinho says, repeating Madhur's last word.

Madhur enters and sees Mrs Coutinho standing with her back to the door, staring at the commode. Her underwear is down by her ankles. She is tapping the commode lightly at various places as if searching for something. Madhur looks at the old woman's face—she appears lost. 'Auntyji, you forgot how to flush kya?' Madhur asks, flushing the commode and quickly pulling up Mrs Coutinho's underwear. She guides her back to bed and makes her lie down. Madhur asks, 'Auntyji, do you want some water? Or tea? Are you feeling faint?'

Mrs Coutinho opens her mouth to say something and stops. She pats Madhur's cheeks with a shaky palm and smiles. 'Sleep,' she says.

'Okay, Auntyji, goodnight.'

It's been a god-awful night, Madhur reminds herself as she is walking to her room, no wonder the old woman is not herself. Her own body feels hot, as if she's in an oven, or still at the parade. Madhur looks in the mirror; her skin is flushed, like a cooked lobster, her clothes are covered in a thin layer of soot and tiny pieces of blackened paper are stuck in her hair. Entering her bathroom, she stands under a cold shower. 'Oh, that's a relief,' she says and sighs. And then, 'Oh shit, I forgot to remove my clothes!' Madhur steps out and flops on the bed in her dripping wet clothes, 'Hey Bhagwan! My body is broken or what? I feel worse than COVID-19 fever.'

Madhur is drifting in and out of sleep, reliving last night's disaster in her head. It feels unreal, like a nightmare, and hopefully the moment she leaves her bed, she will realize that she imagined it all …

She opens her eyes and checks the wall clock, it is now 10.30 a.m.—and a bit odd for the house to be so eerily silent. 'Auntyji must also be sleeping late,' she says to herself, and resolves to take over kitchen duties for the day, giving the old lady a break.

Madhur takes a tray of chai, rotis and aloo sabzi and goes to Mrs Coutinho's bedroom. Placing the tray on a small table, she opens the curtains. Mrs Coutinho turns her face away from the light. 'Auntyji, you have breakfast in bed today. Sleep all day, if you wish.'

Mrs Coutinho stares at the ceiling, ignoring Madhur's presence in the room. Madhur comes closer and gets a strong stench. She lifts the bed cover and sees that Mrs Coutinho has soiled herself. 'No problem, Auntyji. It happens … *koi baat nahi* (no worries). I'll take you to the bathroom and clean you,' she says, extending a hand to help the old lady sit up, simultaneously pulling bedsheets with her other hand. The maid is also late today. Madhur prays for her to walk in through the door and spare her this mess.

Mrs Coutinho continues to stare at the ceiling, holding Madhur's hand limply. Madhur stops what she's doing and pays attention. 'Are you feeling okay, Auntyji?' There's no response from the old lady. Using all her strength, a diminutive Madhur manoeuvres the equally diminutive Mrs Coutinho to an upright position. She stands up but cannot move her limbs. The toilet is just a few metres away, Madhur slowly pushes the old lady inch by inch towards it. It's like pushing a dead weight.

'*Yeh kya hogayaa hain aap ko?* (What has happened to you?) Please don't fall, Auntyji!' Madhur prays. If the old woman breaks a bone, it would further complicate their situation. She aborts the bathroom mission and pushes Mrs Coutinho slowly back to bed. 'Auntyji, tell me what's happening?' Madhur pleads once again, 'Why aren't you walking or talking properly?' Mrs Coutinho smiles weakly. Madhur remembers the tray of food, she tears off a piece of roti, scoops some subzi and puts it in Mrs Coutinho's mouth. The old lady just holds it inside and does not chew. 'Eat it, eat something! Shall I give you chai? A small sip?' Madhur is at her wit's end. She pries open Mrs Coutinho's mouth and retrieves the morsel, lest she choke on it.

It's noon now, half an hour since she found Mrs Coutinho behaving oddly. Madhur gets an idea—she'll check Mrs Coutinho's symptoms on WebMD. But she has no mobile phone! Better to call Karl, she tells herself. Luckily, she remembers his number by heart, having called it frequently on the days preceding his Halloween event. She runs to the rotary dial phone in the sala and calls him.

'Karl, Coutinho Aunty is not feeling well, please come here as fast as you can!'

'Arré, we are also down, men! I have a crazy headache and Jacinta has a bad throat. All that smoke we inhaled … What happened to Aunty Mabel?'

'I don't know, she's not getting up from bed. Her body is stiff.'

'She died awhat!!!'

'No, no! She's awake,' Madhur assures him, 'but she's not talking, she can't move her limbs and she soiled her bed. Something's very wrong.'

'Do one thing, call her family doctor, Dr Fernandes. We'll come in the meantime.'

'My mobile's gone, and his number was in it—wait! Mrs Coutinho has a diary of phone numbers. I'll check in that. You guys please come fast,' Madhur says and disconnects.

Mrs Coutinho keeps the diary inside a drawer of her phone stand. Madhur finds it, calls the doctor and repeats what she said to Karl. The doctor instructs her to pack Mrs Coutinho's clothes and some toiletries in a bag and be ready to admit her to a hospital.

Dr Fernandes, and Karl and Jacinta, arrive at the same time. They enter Mrs Coutinho's bedroom and call out to her separately.

'Mabel?'

'Aunty Mabel?'

She continues staring at the ceiling.

'How long has she been like this?' Dr Fernandes asks Madhur, as he dons his stethoscope to check her.

'I saw her like this at 11.30 a.m.,' says Madhur.

Dr Fernandes flashes a light into Mrs Coutinho's eyes. She blinks but does not register his presence.

'Aunty Mabel was okay last night, when we dropped them after the Narkasur parade. She was a bit shaken—but talking and walking fine,' Jacinta tells the doctor.

'Oh god, you all were there last night! What a mess ... Hospitals are full of burn victims,' the doctor says. Turning to Madhur he asks, 'How was she afterwards? Did she complain of any headache? Body ache?'

'No, but she had slowed down—I mean, Aunty is never slow. Before sleeping she went to the toilet and forgot how to flush—she was searching for the flush lever that was right beside her hand.'

'She couldn't see it?' Karl asks.

'No, it was like she forgot what it was and its purpose,' Madhur clarifies.

'Mabel suffered a massive stroke last night—her pressure is high, her body is functioning erratically as blood is pooling inside her brain. Karl, call 108.' Dr Fernandes tells him to call the government ambulance helpline. 'Actually, let's take her in my car. Madhur, have you packed Mabel's clothes and toiletries for her hospital stay?'

'Yes, doctor.'

'Get it quickly and come with me, and you guys follow in your car,' the doctor instructs them. 'Ambulance guys are stretched because of last night—they'll take too long.'

'Where to? District Hospital?' Karl asks the doctor. 'They're treating last night's victims for free,' he says as they bundle Mrs Coutinho into a bedsheet and place her inside the doctor's car.

'Only burn and injury cases—they won't accept her. Anyway, there's too much chaos in government hospitals right now, let's take her to Vision hospital,' Dr Fernandes says to Karl.

CHAPTER 14

To Everything Turn, Turn, Turn

Karl takes care of formalities and the initial payment required to admit Mrs Coutinho. She is taken directly to the ICU, and while everyone waits outside, it occurs to Madhur that Stella hasn't been told.

Karl sends Stella a message on WhatsApp. She calls immediately and he steps out of the ICU waiting area to answer. Madhur and Jacinta watch from a distance as he speaks animatedly for fifteen minutes. He returns inside looking upset. 'Bloody hell, she's blaming us,' he says to Jacinta. 'Because we took Aunty Mabel to the parade.'

Madhur winces, 'I shouldn't have asked Aunty. She would've slept peacefully at home—it's all my fault.'

'No Maddie, Aunty Coutinho wanted to see the parade. She missed it for so many years because Uncle Godfrey wasn't interested and Stella didn't take her,' Jacinta consoles Madhur.

'I asked Stella to come here. She straightaway said "NO"!' Karl tells Jacinta, 'Babes, I think this is falling on our head. We'll have to take care of her,' he says, looking very conflicted, 'Aai saiba, I have enough on my hands already,' he mutters under his breath.

Dr Fernandes comes out of the ICU and takes Karl aside. 'It's looking very bad,' he says, 'her organs are failing one by one. They want to put her on ventilator. You'll have to sign permission papers,' he tells Karl.

'Why me? Stella should sign. Tell them to wait till she comes from the UK.'

'They cannot wait. And Stella won't be able to come as international flights have not resumed.'

'But this is an emergency! Can't you give her a letter? People are travelling with vaccine certificates.'

'Even if she gets permission, it will take more than a day. We cannot wait even for an hour. So, inform Stella and sign the papers,' Dr Fernandes instructs Karl.

Karl starts to pace, 'What about money? I've already paid an advance of 1 lakh—so expensive these private hospitals are … I asked Stella to send me funds, but she said to wait for some time.'

Jacinta squeezes Karl's shoulder, 'It's your aunt, don't worry about the money. Stella will pay; she's earning in pounds,' she says in her calm, soothing voice. 'Speak to Stella and tell her what the doctors are saying.'

'Babes, why don't you call? I'm afraid I'll lose my temper and say something nasty.' Karl gives his mobile to his wife. She takes it and steps outside into a small terrace area. Walking around the perimeter, mobile glued to her ears, Jacinta nods and listens. After half an hour, she comes inside to the expectant trio of Dr Fernandes, Karl and Madhur.

'No ventilator,' says Jacinta.

'What?' Karl and Madhur respond in unison, Dr Fernandes stays quiet.

'So, let her mother die?' asks Karl.

'She said even her mother wouldn't want it.'

They all turn to look at Dr Fernandes. He clears his throat, 'Actually, Stella's right ... I mean, Mabel's chances are slim. If at all she pulls through, she'll be a vegetable. She'll need help with everything—a twenty-four-hour nurse, oxygen cylinders to breathe, IV fluids to feed. So, is it really worth it? Because we'll just be keeping her body alive. Mabel's gone,' he says.

Madhur starts sobbing. Jacinta is upset. 'Sorry to say this, but Stella's being a bitch,' she says, as everybody looks surprised. 'It's okay to let your mother die peacefully, not put her on ventilator—I understand that. But she wants us—Karl and I—to take money from Madhur, to pay for hospital expenses and the funeral. She cannot come for the funeral also, we have to take care of everything.'

'What?' Madhur is stunned. 'But why should I pay?'

'She says you owe them money, as you didn't pay the security deposit, plus you're paying less rent and eating free food. Also, she was going on and on about how you're using their house to make money with your videos,' Jacinta tells Madhur.

Karl is infuriated, 'Goddamit, the rent was an agreement between Mrs Coutinho and Madhur. What does Stella have to do with it? It's none of her goddamn business. And as for making money from YouTube videos? What does she think? Living with the Coutinho's is like *Living with the Kardashians*? Stupid bitch!'

Dr Fernandes gestures to Karl to calm down. 'I think instead of arguing, you all should say your goodbyes to Mabel. I'll inform them to transfer her from the ICU to a private room—or do you want her in the general ward?' he asks Karl.

'General ward—it's not going to make a difference to Aunty,' he replies.

Dr Fernandes goes inside to confer with the hospital doctors. In an hour's time, Mrs Coutinho is shifted to the general ward. Being a private hospital, it is clean and spacious.

It's 9.00 p.m., and Karl, Jacinta and Madhur have been on their feet for almost eight hours now. In the general ward, a few beds are vacant and they finally get to sit and rest their feet. Karl and Jacinta have only had breakfast, but Madhur has not eaten anything the whole day. They order some food and eat it, sitting beside Mrs Coutinho.

No matter how sombre the mood, the act of eating and sharing food somehow manages to lighten it. Karl cracks a few jokes about Mrs Coutinho, even addressing her—as if she can listen and respond. They all laugh and recollect some happy occasions. Just then Karl's phone rings—it is Stella on a video call. She wants to see her mother before she passes. Karl holds the phone and shows her. Stella cries profusely, speaking in Konkani to her mother. Jacinta translates for Madhur.

'Stella, come to Goa. We'll keep her body in a refrigerated coffin till you arrive,' Karl says to her, 'You missed your dad's funeral because you had exams. That time you said, "Daddy will understand, he wanted me to study hard." What's your excuse now? And don't say COVID-19—my friend just returned from the UK, three days ago.'

Stella hesitates, 'Karl, I've lost my job—it's been a year. My husband has been jobless for even longer—since Brexit. He used to drive his truck through EU countries … I feel ashamed to say this—but we've used up all our savings and are currently living on social security,' she says, looking crestfallen. 'I hope schools open again—only the senior teachers are allowed to take online classes—but it's doubtful. NHS says COVID-19 is here to stay.'

'How come Aunty Mabel didn't tell me?' Karl asks, looking surprised.

'I didn't tell Mummy. But you know what, I'm done feeling ashamed. I don't care what you all think of me—it is what it is,' she says.

Everybody bids goodbye to a tearful Stella, and Karl ends the video call. He rolls his eyes, and Jacinta detects a hint of a smile. She looks at him questioningly.

'Bloody hell,' he starts. 'Why do Goans go to the UK? They think they'll make tons of money by earning in pounds. Hehh! The minute there's some problem, those goras fire us Indians first! Stella gave me big talks about how I was wasting my life in Goa, and now who's paying her mother's hospital bills? And later, funeral,' Karl says making a sign of the cross. 'In the time it took her to be an assistant teacher, I am running a media business. What ego! She went to teach English to the Brits! Teach here in Goa, no? If you are so good, let the kids over here benefit. She's living in poverty now.'

'But even the poor in the UK are better off than the middle-class in Goa,' Jacinta reminds Karl. Turning to Madhur, she says, 'You know, Karl was always compared to Stella by his mother—Karl's mother and Aunty Mabel are sisters. Karl and Stella studied in the same class. Stella was the class topper, and Karl was the backbencher. Karl finally gets to one-up Stella.' Turning to Karl she says, 'Unfortunately, your mother is not alive to see this.'

Madhur smiles weakly. She has had one eye constantly on the monitors surrounding Mrs Coutinho's bed. They've been instructed to call a nurse if anything flashes red and beeps. As Karl and Jacinta reminisce about school days, Madhur digs into the duffel bag she's carrying and pulls out Mrs Coutinho's toiletry kit. She takes out a comb and fixes her silver-grey hair—the old lady likes to be tip-top always. She powders Mrs Coutinho's face around her oxygen mask, even as she breathes hard with wheezing sounds.

'Auntyji, it's time for our night cap,' she says to Mrs Coutinho. 'Cheers to you.' Madhur holds a plastic glass of water aloft. 'Thank you for everything, Auntyji, you looked after me like I was your daughter—you did more for me than my own mother,' Madhur says, tears streaking her face. She holds Mrs Coutinho's hand in hers and squeezes it. 'We'll miss you—I will miss you a lot, but you have to go, Auntyji. Don't suffer any more.'

Madhur's body shakes as she tries to control her sobs, aware that they are in a general ward. Jacinta rubs her back to console her. 'Maddie, I doubt Stella ever spent as much time as you do with Aunty Mabel. You make her happy. She is fortunate to have you as a tenant.'

The monitors start flashing red and beeping maniacally. Patients on neighbouring beds crane their necks and look worried. Two nurses and a young doctor come running to check Mrs Coutinho's pulse. It is not required—her heartbeat monitor has flatlined. A senior doctor comes by and checks his watch. He calls her death, '11.45 p.m., 2 November,' he says, as Madhur, Karl and Jacinta look on.

CHAPTER 15

Funeral Blues

Mrs Coutinho's body is kept in an open coffin in the sala of Casa Coutinho, surrounded by flower wreaths and candles. People from the vaddo have been trickling in since morning. Madhur makes herself useful by keeping a live video feed going—for Stella in the UK, and relatives and friends living in Portugal.

This is Madhur's first time attending a Catholic funeral; she has only seen them before in movies. Not knowing what is expected of her, she stands quietly in a corner. Many neighbours look at her with suspicion, calling her 'Delhi girl', like it's a bad word. But some approach her and hug her fondly. 'You were like a daughter to Mabel,' one old lady says. 'After Stella went to the UK, and her husband Godfrey died, she was so lonely in this big house. Thank God, you came to live with her. So happy you made her—I could hear her singing again!'

Jacinta calls Madhur, gesturing her to come into the kitchen 'Maddie, show me where the trays are,' she says. 'I have to serve tea and snacks to the guests.'

Madhur opens the cupboard with the chinaware from Macau that Mrs Coutinho had kept for special occasions. 'Aunty did not use these plates and trays,' she tells Jacinta. 'They are more than 200 years old, and nobody has used them! What are we going to do now—send them to a museum? She used those La Opala plates and bowls, because they are unbreakable.' Madhur points to the wooden cabinet above the kitchen platform, where the everyday-use cutlery and dinner sets are stored. 'And now, without using these plates, she's gone ...' Madhur starts sniffling. Jacinta hugs her tight. 'Aunty Mabel was so lucky to have you. I'm so sorry you didn't get to celebrate Diwali. Goa ruined it for you, na?' Jacinta consoles her.

And it dawns on Madhur that Diwali was the day before.

But the festival of death overshadowed the festival of light— only because of the stupidity of the living. She thinks of all the people who got injured at the parade; they may have suffered a more painful death than Mrs Coutinho. For some survivors, the nightmare that began on the eve of Diwali, continues, as they battle between life and death in government hospital wards. Madhur has no inkling of the death count—she's not had time to read newspapers or watch TV news. And without her mobile phone, she feels rudderless. The lack of crackers and festivity all around her, tells her that Diwali is definitely cancelled this year.

The mass and burial are scheduled for 12 noon at St. Anne's Church, Parra. Madhur finds it ironic that she will finally enter the Parra Church to do a Live YouTube feed—not for social media likes, but for a funeral. She has always felt that the church expected something bigger from her.

At 11.45 a.m., with the sound of church bells tolling, a solemn procession winds its way out of Almeida vaddo, followed by a brass band playing the dirge. Karl has used his contacts to get the best jazz musicians in Goa. Madhur films everything with a borrowed phone—Karl's (he has asked her to keep his old iPhone till she can afford a new one). Stella, meanwhile, makes several suggestions and complaints as she tries to stage-manage the funeral via the video. Karl brushes her off—and he can—he's paying for it. Mrs Coutinho is laid to rest beside her husband, Godfrey Coutinho. All the graves at the St. Anne's Church cemetery are bedecked with flowers, still fresh from the All Souls Day celebrations the night before. As people start to leave the cemetery, Jacinta pulls Madhur aside. 'Come home and have lunch with us,' she says. 'Stay for a few days. Please don't stay alone in that house.'

'Thank you for the kind offer, Jacinta. I don't know what I would've done without you and Karl,' Madhur says. 'I'll just have lunch and return to Casa Coutinho. It's not good to keep the house locked and empty tonight. And I want to light a diya for Coutinho Aunty's *aatma* (soul). It's a Hindu ritual, I know, but I feel like I should do it. Aunty will not mind, I'm sure.'

Karl pats Madhur's back, 'Okay, Maddie, you do what feels right. But eat lunch and go back. The caterer has sent over some good food.' Turning to Jacinta, he says, 'Babe, let's pack her some food for a few days too. Or else she won't eat. I know her.'

Karl and Jacinta Mascarenhas stay in Guirim in a modern villa just ten minutes' drive from Casa Coutinho. The food is already laid out in a buffet when they enter. Karl opens a bottle of rosé wine and pours out three glasses. Passing a glass each to Jacinta and Madhur, he raises a toast, 'To Tia Mabel. Homemaker, dressmaker, great cook and even better singer! A super landlady to our friend Madhur, bestest aunt to Jacinta and me. She lived well, and may her life be an inspiration to us all.'

They help themselves to the delicious spread, and move to sit in the hall and eat.

'So, Maddie, how are you doing?' Karl asks.

'I don't know,' Madhur replies. 'I feel so much sadder than when my own Dad died. Actually, I just blocked his death out, I think. But here, in Goa, I cannot do that. In a big city one can hide behind work—there are so many other distractions too. Here, there are none,' Madhur ponders.

Karl smiles. 'Maddie, I want to ask you a few things, also because Stella wants to know. But you can take your own time to decide,' he says. Madhur immediately straightens up, sensing an important conversation.

'Have you thought about where you're going to stay, now that Aunty Mabel is no more?"

'Shit, I haven't thought of it …' Madhur replies.

'I thought that maybe you'd want to return to Delhi, to your mom. Goa's been rough on you, right?'

'I can't—don't want to go back,' Madhur says, feeling her throat clogging up.

'See, based on my conversations with Stella, here's the problem I anticipate,' Karl says while sipping his wine. 'She wants to sell Casa Coutinho.'

Madhur's face crumbles.

'Not right away, I think. It's a long procedure. She'll have to come to Goa first, then it'll take a year or more for the house to be transferred to her name as Goa property laws are different from rest of the country. Besides, due to COVID-19 lockdowns, the courts have a backlog of cases,' Karl explains. 'As I see it, you have two options. You can either continue staying at Casa Coutinho or—'

Madhur interrupts, 'Can I transfer my rent to Stella?'

'No rent to be paid for now,' he replies.

Madhur is flabbergasted. 'What do you mean? She was complaining that I pay less than the standard rates. How will she let me stay rent-free?'

'Instead of paying rent, Stella wants you to use the money to look after the house. Basically, she wants you to be the caretaker and keep the house in a decent condition, till she comes to Goa. And I've been asked to look for buyers.'

Madhur doesn't understand Stella's offer. But she trusts Karl to give her the right advice, 'What does it mean for me?' she asks.

'Maddie, do you have any idea how much Aunty Mabel spent on the house, on a monthly basis—just running costs,' he asks her. 'I'm sure she kept an accounts book.'

'I don't know, Karl, she didn't tell me about it. And why would I ask such a thing? I'm a tenant.'

Jacinta nods knowingly and says, 'We're asking because Stella says that the cost is minimal. She says her mother didn't use her pounds remittance from the UK and saved it in fixed deposits. She managed the monthly expenses with the rent you paid.'

'But Auntyji visited the bank every month, sometimes twice! I assumed that she was withdrawing the money sent by Stella, at least some of it. I paid her in cash, and she used it for grocery and drinks mostly. And I don't know … maybe she gave some money to an orphanage every month, when she went there.'

'The Thivim Orphanage? Nah, she just gave her time,' Karl clarifies.

Jacinta turns to Karl and says, 'Forget all this. There are too many complications. I know Stella is lying. Why get Maddie involved in their family matters? Let's help her find a new place instead. In Parra itself, if she prefers that.'

Karl turns to Maddie, 'And that's the second option. I help you find a small flat in a new building or a room with an attached bathroom—with geyser, AC and all—within the same rent bracket. Jacinta is right, it's better if you move out.'

'If you think that's best,' Madhur says, feeling her heart grow heavy. She pushes her plate of food away, with the food untouched. So is her glass of wine.

'You'll not be asked to leave immediately,' Karl reassures her, 'Stay in the house this month. You are entitled to a full month's notice, and Stella just raised this issue today. We can start looking for a new place tomorrow. Don't worry, Maddie, it'll be okay,' he says.

Karl drops Madhur to Casa Coutinho at 4.00 p.m. She opens the main door and enters an empty house. The smell of flowers and burnt wax is lingering in the air. The first thing that catches her eye is a large photo of Mrs Coutinho on the sala wall. Running to her bedroom, Madhur flings herself on the bed and falls asleep immediately, the sleep deficit of the last two days finally catching up with her.

It is pitch dark when she awakens. She looks at the iPhone beside her. It says 9.00 p.m., 3 November. Switching on all the lights in the passageway, she goes to the kitchen. Madhur finds Mrs Coutinho's oil *ginni*—a small steel utensil with a thin, long spout—and pours some oil into a *mitti ka diya* (clay diya) she had bought for Diwali. Taking cotton from a first aid kit kept on the fridge, she rolls out a wick, dabs its tip with oil and lights it. Holding the diya reverentially in both hands, Madhur walks to the big portrait of Mrs Coutinho and places it on the floor directly below it. She kneels down and says a small prayer—Mrs Coutinho's night prayer—which she now knows by heart.

She gets up and sits on a sofa facing the portrait. Feeling refreshed after a five-hour long nap, Madhur doesn't know what to do with rest of the night. She observes the other portraits on the wall—generations of departed family members, and

Mrs Coutinho's portrait is the latest addition to that lot. She gets goosebumps thinking of all the dead Coutinhos watching her and runs to the kitchen. The kitchen feels like a safe space. She heats up the food Jacinta has packed, puts it all in one bowl and goes to her room to eat. Opening her balcony, she drags a chair to sit outside.

Everything looks dark, the air heavy with a sense of foreboding, now that Madhur is all alone in the cavernous confines of Casa Coutinho. Familiar sights appear frightening to her. The old villa is surrounded by ten ancient mango trees, one very old and tall silk cotton tree and a grove of 100 coconut trees. Thick foliage hangs over the villa, an arms' distance from where Madhur is seated. This green canopy is home to a host of avian and animal life. She tries hard to ignore their cackling, cawing, chirping, hissing and wing-flapping sounds interrupting the still air. How come she never heard all this before? Mrs Coutinho's constant chatter, lilting laughter, her soulful renditions of Konkani and Portuguese songs had kept the darkness and the night sounds at bay. Madhur recollects a haunting melody…

Ravom yeta mojean jeu nastonam,
Sarum yeta rath nido nastonam,
Punn ravonk zainam mojean tuka, poi nastonam
Ugddas yeta ut'tam bostonam …[4]

---

4   I can live without eating
    Pass the night without sleeping
    But I cannot live without seeing you
    I remember you every moment of the day
    –Tujo Mog, by Lorna Cordeiro (Nightingale of Goa)

Now there is no protection. Madhur feels exposed. Lifting her gaze from her food bowl, she glances at her own reflection on a window-pane, and panics as if she's seen a ghost. She rushes inside to the dining room. Sitting at the table, she catches her breath, and remembers all those times she did not join Mrs Coutinho for dinner. Madhur feels a hint of the loneliness Countinho Aunty must have felt, eating alone at a table set for two.

Staring into her food bowl, she realizes she knows exactly what to do in order to feel better. Madhur fetches cutlery, table mats and napkins, and sets the table properly, just the way Mrs Coutinho liked it. Next, she lights the candles on the stand and places fresh flowers in the round vase. She piles food on a plate and, finally, sits down to eat her meal.

CHAPTER 16

All Is Not, Well, Water

Mrs Coutinho's maid quits two days after the funeral. Amita Gaonkar, the maid, feels no affinity towards Madhur. She collects her last salary from Madhur and leaves.

'I will not take orders from an "outsider",' she tells Karl, when he calls her to enquire about her quitting without any notice. 'I'll return to work only when Stella baby comes back home,' she declares.

Karl guffaws, 'Your Stella baby is going to sell the house, and for the amount she's asking, she'll get an "outside" buyer only. The filthy rich kind. You come to work then, okay? Let them flog you from morning till midnight. When people are nice, y'all don't respect them,' he says, ending the call.

He calls Madhur next. 'Just keep your room clean and forget about the rest of the house. Let Stella clean it via a zoom call.'

Madhur feels remorseful. 'Aunty wouldn't have liked this. The house was her heart and soul.'

'Aye, you relax, haan! This is the story of every old Goan house. Maybe that's why there are so many ghosts in Goa, especially near old, broken-down homes—and most of them are female ghosts. You women really invest your lives into your homes. No wonder y' all can't let go of them even after death,' he says and guffaws.

Madhur does not find it funny at all. 'Don't say that! I'm still living in the house!'

'Chill re, there are no ghosts. I was joking,' Karl quickly reassures her. 'By the way, you are always welcome to stay at our place. You know that, right?'

'I know, thank you,' she says and ends the call.

Madhur immediately starts scrolling through property websites on her laptop, fervently hoping to discover a kind soul like Mrs Coutinho. There are quite a few options available in her meagre budget, but they are mostly single rooms or studio apartments furnished with cheap metal or plastic furniture. Maybe that's what she'll have to manage with now. Anything that resembles Casa Coutinho is way out of her league. She pauses for a moment to thank Mrs Coutinho for welcoming her into her villa and life; a world so completely different from Kalkaji LIG homes.

Her six-month lucky streak is now coming to an end. '*Koi baat nahin* (No worries),' Madhur says aloud, 'I managed in Kalkaji, na?'

If anything, her stay at Casa Coutinho is an aberration, she concurs.

Six months ago, Madhur had seen Casa Coutinho listed on a property rental site. It was out of her budget—₹25,000 per month for a single room. She had just arrived from Delhi and was staying in a cheap hotel at Arpora. Casa Coutinho showed up as less than two kilometres on the app. It looked beautiful in the photos posted on the site. Madhur had never been to a Goan-Portuguese villa before, and she was intrigued. So that evening, on an impulse, she took a stroll to check it out. If not anything, she would get nice pictures for Instagram.

Mrs Coutinho had welcomed her with tea and biscuits, asking her all kinds of questions regarding her family, her work, her Delhi life and some random questions like, 'Have you been to the Republic Day parade?'

Madhur had seen it on TV, because *kaun jayega Rajpath* (who will go to Rajpath)?

'Haanji,' she had said to Mrs Coutinho, 'Every year I go to see the parade.'

'You know, the Goa State Float is made by my third cousin, from my father's side!' Mrs Coutinho had said to her.

'It's the best!' Madhur had said honestly.

By the end of the conversation, Mrs Coutinho knew everything there was to know about her. As Madhur got up to leave, Mrs Coutinho asked her how much rent she could afford. Madhur was too embarrassed to quote a figure.

'I absolutely cannot go below ₹10,000,' Mrs Coutinho had said. 'So ... what do you say?'

Madhur shuts her laptop and goes to the kitchen to make some chai and breakfast for herself. It's been four days since the funeral, and she hasn't cooked at all. Jacinta's food packets are still going strong. All she has to do is heat and eat them, but even that is an effort. The kitchen window looks out to the coconut grove. At the far right, about ten meters from the kitchen, is the outside bathroom attached to a well. Madhur takes her cup of chai and steps out. She opens the bathroom door and sees a large copper pot sitting on charred firewood. She lifts the lid and sees that there is some water inside. The last bathwater Mrs Coutinho had heated before she died. Madhur has been taking cold baths ever since.

She walks to the well and peers inside. The water is at least ten meters below. Somehow, she expected it to be within arm's reach. She looks up at the pulley attached to a wooden truss, and the long rope tied to it is lying outside. Her Mummyji would know how to draw water from a well like this. Madhur wonders if she should call her and ask. 'Google zindabad,' she whispers to herself, and starts looking for a video. She finds several, and watches a few. 'Ha! This is easy,' she says, triumphantly. Feeling confident, she throws the thick rope with a copper pot attached, into the well.

Alas, her execution of the seemingly simple steps is not so smooth. After thirty minutes of struggling, she barely manages to draw out two litres of water. The pot keeps tipping over and spilling almost all the water back into the well, as she heaves it up. Defeated, Madhur returns to the kitchen, and fills tap water into a large steel utensil and places it on the stove for heating. 'I tried, Auntyji!' she says aloud. 'But it takes years of practise to do it like you and Amita.'

Auntyji and Mummyji would have gotten along well had they met. Both of them had grown up in a village, though Mrs Coutinho was older, more modern and sophisticated in her ways. Then again, maybe not, ponders Madhur. Their similarities seem superficial, but their core values are polar opposites, she concludes. After the funeral, Karl and Jacinta were curious to know why she didn't want to return to be with Mummyji. Madhur could not explain her reasons to them. How could she tell them that her Dad was the buffer between Mummyji and her? Without him, she was afraid they would be at each other's throats all day long.

Mummyji disapproved of everything Madhur did, or did not do. There was no way of pleasing her. Like that time immediately after the lockdown. Madhur was stuck at home, as was the entire world, doing exactly what the rest of the world was doing.

'Why are you just sitting around? *Kuch kaam kar!* (Do some work!)' Mummyji screamed every day.

'*Kya karoon?* All the offices are shut, Mummyji. Even if I wanted to, I can't work ... bloody hell, *méréy* boutique *ka band bajaa diya iss COVID-19 né* (this COVID-19 screwed up my boutique plans)!'

'*Tu pooréy din mobile pé kya dékhti réhti hain?* (What do you keep watching on your mobile?)' Mummyji asked.

'Netflix! *Aur kya? Poori duniya yeh hi kar rahi hain. Zindagi toh jhannd hogayi hain, Mummyji.* (What else? The whole world is watching it. Our lives have gone for a toss, Mummyji.)'

Of course, Madhur helped out in the kitchen, shopped for groceries, sanitised every object bought and ran all the outdoor errands. Mummyji, however, expected more of her—what it was, was never communicated clearly.

One day, Mummyji's new grouse was, 'Why didn't Madhur study medicine? Why couldn't she be a doctor or a nurse—at least she'd be out working during COVID-19. What use was her fashion degree? *Kuch nahin toh safaai karmachari banti.* (She could have become a sweeper, if nothing else.)

Moving away from Delhi, Madhur has finally put physical and emotional distance between Mummyji and herself. They can love and respect each other from afar. There's no way she will go back and ruin this.

Lost in her thoughts, Madhur sits on the backdoor steps. The water on the stove will take half an hour to boil—unlike firewood, which barely takes ten minutes. It's 10.30 a.m., the sun is overhead, but the trees provide shade in the backyard and keep it cool. It's the second week of November and some of the older neighbours have brought out their sweaters. Madhur observes an old aunty sweeping her backyard in the distance, fully kitted in a sweater, shawl and monkey cap. '*Koshem aaha? Borem mugo?* (How are you? All good?)' she shouts out to Madhur. 'Yes, *borem, borem* (good, good)!' Madhur shouts back and waves.

For a Delhiite, the Goan winter can hardly be called a winter. The temperatures never dip below double digits. At best, she feels a slight nip in the air whilst riding her scooter early mornings or at night. She remembers Mrs Coutinho scolding her, 'It's not the temperature, my dear girl. We have a wet climate. The morning and evening mist can give you a bad cold. Just cover your head, nose and your ears—the rest can stay uncovered, if you want.' Madhur giggles imagining herself riding a scooter stark naked, save for a monkey cap on her head. 'Such a cartoon you were, Auntyji, *ab mujhe kaun hasaayega* (who will make me laugh now).'

While walking in the backyard, she notices pink flowers on the ground, a little further from the coconut grove. 'Arre wah! Mrs Coutinho's Semal tree is in full bloom!' Madhur runs to inspect the flowers, suddenly feeling nostalgic about Delhi parks. The silk cotton tree, or Semal, is a common feature in Delhi too. It sheds all its leaves to herald the onset of winter, and covers itself with dark pink, cup-shaped flowers. Madhur stands on a carpet of pink petals and looks up. The Semal is as tall as a six-story building, towering above all other vegetation. The rain rich climate of Goa makes them taller than the Semals of Delhi. Several birds are chattering away on its branches, feasting on the nectar contained within the flowers, dropping the exhausted ones purposely on her head.

Mrs Coutinho's Semal tree looks ancient—it has a smooth trunk. The young trees have thorns all over their bark. This tree must be nearly 300 years old, or older, maybe? She circumambulates its wide base of buttress roots. The gaps between the roots are big enough for a person to fit inside. Madhur lowers herself and curls up in a foetal position in one such gap. The moist mud immediately coats her exposed skin, but she doesn't mind. She imagines what it would feel like if the Semal roots closed in on her, clutching her in a tight embrace. Then she would become one with the tree. Its snaking roots—thicker than elephant feet—would easily swallow her, leaving no trace.

The wet earth smell fills her nostrils. Madhur opens her eyes and looks up at the wide canopy of pink flowers against the blue sky, her body awash with a sudden feeling of peacefulness. Like she is cocooned in the warm, fecund embrace of a mother. A matriarch, like Mrs Coutinho.

'Am I missing Delhi kya?' she mutters. Well, she is—even though it hurts to admit it. And, not all of it, just the gardens, the trees and the cool winters. Definitely not the people, though.

She suddenly remembers the water on the stove. Dusting the mud off herself, she gets up and runs inside to the kitchen. The water has boiled itself down to half its quantity. Using a thick towel, she lifts the utensil and pours the hot water into a bucket. While taking a bath, steaming water running over her body, she contemplates about Stella's proposal: to continue living in Casa Coutinho till it gets sold. The more she thinks about it, the better she feels. Who knows, maybe there'll be a fourth wave of COVID-19—delaying Stella's travel to Goa even further.

CHAPTER 17

Ghosts of Weddings Past

Madhur calls Karl and tells him she'd like to go along with Stella's proposal.

'Did you find the accounts book?' he asks her.

'Actually, how do I say this ... I feel uncomfortable going through Aunty's things. If Stella searches for it, then it's fine.'

'You better not wait till Stella finds it. Look, Maddie, you need this information. What if it takes ₹25,000, or more, to run the house for a month? It's a big house. Stella used to send money every month—even when she lost her job. There are electricity bills—'

'Only ₹350 to ₹400 max, every month,' Madhur interrupts, 'I know because Aunty made me pay them online.'

'How so less?' Karl is surprised.

'No ACs, geysers, mixer-grinder or washing machine. And more than half the house is closed shut, only three rooms are used,' says Madhur.

'Okay, but you'll need a new maid, and she may charge double. You will need to hire gardeners to come in every week. The house and the compound wall will need a fresh coat of paint by December, even though it's still mourning period and Christmas won't be celebrated. You'll also need to call the coconut-plucker, on a quarterly basis, and sell those coconuts, keep an account and send the logs to Stella. There's a LOT of work.'

'I'll manage! I tried drawing well-water yesterday,' Madhur tells him excitedly, 'I saw a tutorial on YouTube and did it. Agreed, I need to practise more, but I will keep trying till I get it. I'll manage everything else in the same manner, slowly, slowly,' she says.

There is no response from Karl, and it seems like the call has been disconnected. 'Hello?' She asks.

'Why are you doing this?' Karl responds.

Madhur senses frustration in his tone. She doesn't know what to say.

'Why?' he asks again. 'What are you trying to prove, Maddie? I know it's fun the first few times—drawing water from a well, lighting a woodfire ... I'm sure it makes great Instagram Reels, but can you do it day in and day out, for over a year? Maddie, real life is not an Instagram Reel. Real life is twenty-four hours, 365 days, and not just a few seconds.'

'You know I don't do Instagram Reels anymore,' Madhur replies in a pained voice.

Karl continues, 'So you could install a geyser. But I'm certain that old house's wiring can't support geysers and ACs—that's why Aunty Mabel didn't do it. Then there are the servants. Aunty Mabel had a command over them. They did her work out of loyalty to her—I'm sure she hadn't increased their wages in the last few years. They've been working with that family for generations. Godfrey Coutinho was a big bhaatcar.'

'A whatcar?' Madhur asks.

'A landowner. He had an abundance of property, land and resources, so he worked pro-bono for poor people,' Karl explains. 'The maid, the gardener, the coconut-plucker—they all work for lesser wages out of gratitude. They are "mundkars"—tenants, of the Coutinho family. They live on Uncle Godfrey's land—some of which he has gifted away to them. Uncle and Aunty are like gods for them.'

'Okay.'

'I don't think you'll be able to manage. Not without Aunty Mabel.'

'But I can try,' insists Madhur.

'My dear, it's not about trying, it's an attitude. Even Jacinta couldn't handle the maids in our old house, the way my mom did. But when we built our new house, Jacinta's attitude changed. Because it was her house and her maids—do you get what I'm saying, Maddie?'

'*Thoda-thodasa*. (A little bit.)'

'Good, because there's something you should know about Stella ... no matter how well you keep Casa Coutinho, she'll find faults and bleed you dry. Just like she has done with me. My advice to you is—don't deal with her. She is not Aunty Mabel!'

'If you say so, Karl.'

'Maddie, Casa Coutinho is prime property. Stella listed it on a property website just two days ago—with my contact details—and five buyers have already shown up at my office with wads of cash to buy it outright. All Delhi parties ... And they kept insisting. No matter how much I told them that it's not mine to sell, they wouldn't budge!'

'Oh.'

'I told them that it will take at least a year before it can be sold. So out of those five buyers, only three are willing to wait. But what I'm saying is, Maddie, if you stay at Casa Coutinho, your stay will be temporary and uncertain. You could be asked to leave any moment ... why live like that?' he implores. 'I'm also looking into how the whole transfer and sale process can be expedited—not for Stella's sake—for mine. I'm getting a 2 per cent cut for my work,' Karl informs her. 'It will cover my expenses at the hospital and the funeral. Do you see how she's making me work to get my own money back? I have to find buyers for the house and broker a good deal just so I can get my own money ... that bloody bitch! There's no winning with her... I hope someday Karma fucks her bad!'

After the call, Madhur feels despondent. She enters her room and surveys her belongings. She has sold only twelve of the fifty Madfashions outfits she had brought to Goa. Apart from this, she had her laptop and mobile equipment, and her photography accessories. She looks at her outfits, hanging neatly on old fashioned wooden hangers, inside the ornately carved teakwood wardrobe in her room. The musky smell of teakwood always makes her heady, and she feels like she's in a forest. More than 200 years old, the wardrobe provides a regal backdrop for her outfits. She pulls out all her clothes, leaving only three on the hangers. Stepping back, she admires them from afar. Perhaps some spot lighting inside would do the trick, she tells herself. Madhur makes a mental note to use an antique wardrobe to display clothes, rather than mannequins. Or how about mannequins inside the wardrobe? Each wardrobe will display a different setting—like, one can have mannequins draped with short, red and white polka dotted dresses, seated at a table and having coffee. 'I must write down these ideas before I forget,' she tells herself, only to remember that she no longer styles fashion shoots or designs window displays.

As the 7.00 p.m. church bell starts ringing, Madhur realizes that three hours have passed since her call with Karl, and she has made little to no progress with her packing. All her clothes are lying scattered on the floor and on her bed. Madhur goes to the altar and recites the Angelus followed by Hanuman Chalisa, and returns to her room to resume packing in earnest.

Bent over the clothes and sifting through them, Madhur catches a blur of white in her peripheral vision. She lifts her head and watches a trail of white silk fabric gliding on the floor outside her room. Perplexed, she gets up and goes to investigate. But the hallway, rooms and kitchen are empty. 'Did I imagine it?' Madhur wonders aloud and returns to her room. After a few seconds of packing, she hears a soft rustling of clothes, followed by footsteps on the wooden staircase.

With her heart beating in her throat, Madhur bravely decides to follow the sound of the steps. She climbs the staircase saying, 'Hello, *kaun hai?* (Who's there?)' Moving towards Godfrey's office, she stops in the corridor and waits till her eyes adjust to the darkness. There it is again, shimmering in the dark, a trail of a white silk wedding gown. Somebody is entering Mrs Coutinho's master bedroom. Madhur steps inside the room just in time to see the trail vanish inside a shut wardrobe. She knocks on the wardrobe, '*Baahar niklo!* (Come out!)' she demands. There's no answer at first. And then Mrs Coutinho's voice whispers in her ears, 'Madhur, wake up!'

Madhur opens her eyes abruptly, sweat pouring down her face and heart beating a mile-a-minute. She looks around and realizes that she fell asleep on the floor between her two suitcases. Stretching her knotted body, she gets up and sleeps properly on her bed.

Next morning, she takes Mrs Coutinho's key bunch and climbs the wooden staircase to the master bedroom. She opens the wardrobe, retrieves Mrs Coutinho's wedding gown and packs it inside her suitcase; thanking the old lady for sending her a sign to keep it.

PART III

CHAPTER 18

Fuchsia Fashion

Madhur shortlists five properties and shares the listings with Karl. He responds immediately to her WhatsApp, 'I know two of the owners, their studio apartments look nothing like the pictures they've posted,' his message says. 'But check out the other three, I'll come along with you, if you want.'

Madhur likes a studio apartment in a bright yellow building in Mont de Guirim, called Shubhangi Niwas. It is a fifteen-minute walk from Karl's place, and the apartment is furnished modestly, but is still a little outside her budget. 'You are close to my home and office,' Karl tries to convince her, 'Jacinta and I will always be around if you need anything.' They make the final negotiations with the owner and Madhur pays an advance.

'I'll accompany you tomorrow for the agreement, and also pick up your things. Will your luggage fit inside my SUV, or do you need a truck?' he jokes.

'I just have two suitcases,' Madhur replies ruefully.

'Fine then, tonight will be your last at Casa Coutinho,' he says, 'and I'll inform Stella that you're moving out.'

Madhur parks her scooter one last time outside the main entrance of Casa Coutinho. She enters the house, remembering the first time she had stepped inside. Walking around the sala, she gently caresses the furniture, antique vases, velvet lounge sofas, teakwood and mahogany display cupboards, all the framed photographs on the wall, as if acknowledging them. Every object feels alive to her touch.

Walking into her room, she sees her suitcases in one corner, her bed draped with new sheets—the old sheets are washed and put away in Mrs Coutinho's cupboard. Her wardrobe is open and empty. Madhur inhales the intoxicating wood smell one last time—her new studio apartment has a Godrej metal almirah, just like her home in Kalkaji. She walks around her room, opening the bedstand drawers, opening the wardrobe again, entering the bathroom to check if anything is left behind, opening the wardrobe again. She latches the two windows in her room, bolts the balcony door, checks underneath the bed and opens the wardrobe again. Glancing into the oval mirror on her wardrobe, she sees tears roll down her cheeks.

Next morning, Karl arrives at 9.00 a.m. to pick her luggage and stand as witness to her rental agreement. Madhur makes a cup of chai for him and turns off the LPG cylinder. While he is loading her luggage, she takes a quick last look at the house and locks the main door. She hands over the keys to Karl, feeling a huge sense of relief and sadness. Some neighbours come outside to wish her goodbye, while a few stare from their windows. Madhur gets on her scooter and rides out of Parra through the *Dear Zindagi* road, passing a horde of people posing under coconut trees.

They are at Shubhangi Niwas in fifteen minutes. As Madhur is unloading her bags, a young girl—roughly the same age as her, comes by and offers to help.

'I'm Chaitali, you must be Madhur. Baba said you're also a fashion designer. Here, let me carry this for you.'

'Hello Chaitali, nice to meet you. No, no, don't worry. I'll take them,' Madhur says, but cannot stop her from carrying one of the suitcases up the staircase. Karl shrugs his shoulders and says, 'My job is done. You've got a new friend now. Come by in the evening if you feel like it,' he says, giving her a hug.

Chaitali helps Madhur settle into her room and continues to hang around. Madhur waits politely for her to leave, but she flits about showing her how everything works. 'That's the fan switch ... that's the geyser switch ... shut the terrace at all times, or langurs can enter the building ...'

'Hey Madhur, which batch were you in,' she stops and asks suddenly.

'Haan?'

'You went to NIFT, na? Baba told me.'

'Yes, I graduated in 2018.'

'Oh really? You know, I would've been your batchmate,' she says excitedly. 'But aai-baba refused to send me to Delhi ...you know that Nirbhaya case? I gave up my seat at NIFT Delhi and pursued fashion design from Sophia Polytechnic, Mumbai. I have lots of relatives in Mumbai ... so.'

'Oh nice! But there is an NIFT in Mumbai also.'

'It's in Navi Mumbai, Khargar ... very far. And in Mumbai, Sophia's is the best,' Chaitali says.

'Haan ... I've heard. So where do you work now—I mean, are you working?'

'Yes, yes. I have my own boutique,' Chaitali says and runs to the balcony. 'See there? That's my boutique.'

Madhur goes out and sees a bright, fuchsia pink, double-storeyed garage-like structure, diagonally across the road from their building. It has a huge signboard on the entrance with 'Chaitali' written in blue against white. A dark red bougainvillea shrub frames a blue entrance door. She wonders how she missed such a bright and cheerful shop.

'Very nice,' Madhur compliments Chaitali, despite the pang in her heart.

'Thanks,' says Chaitali. 'I'm so happy you're living with us now. You must be a really big designer. I've seen your Insta and YouTube videos.'

'Accha? You already googled me? I don't know about being a big designer and all ... And, honestly, I haven't designed anything in the last one year—or more.'

'Because you're busy vlogging?' Chaitali asks.

'No, not because of that. I came to Goa to sell clothes, via my fashion blog ... but it didn't work out well. I had approached some boutiques too. But I wasn't getting my prices, and they wanted huge mark ups. So, now I'm doing set design and graphics for a friend who is into events.'

'You can display your clothes at my boutique! I'll just take five to ten percent.'

'Oh! Thank you, I'll think about it.' Saying so, she politely steers Chaitali out.

Madhur flops on her narrow, single bed, and sighs. Her bed is near the balcony; and she can see rice fields stretching up to a distant hill. A tiny, white-washed chapel nestles in the midst of an ocean of green stalks, rippling like waves in the breeze. She breathes deeply and shifts her gaze back inside, to her room. It is compact like any modern studio apartment, with a tiny kitchen area that has a meter-long granite platform. A single burner gas stove is kept on top of this platform, with a cylinder positioned below. A small maroon fridge stands beside the platform, with a microwave on top. The TV monitor on the wall opposite her bed is the size of her laptop. A dark blue Godrej almirah is beside her bed, near the bathroom. There is an AC and a fan too. Inside the tiny bathroom, there's a commode, a washbasin, geyser and a shower. The redeeming factor is the balcony—it runs the entire length of the room, opening it out to vistas of field and sky. If it wasn't for the balcony, she would have felt claustrophobic in this tiny room, filled with stuff that should ideally be spread out across two or three rooms.

Her studio apartment has all the conveniences required to live comfortably. What more can anyone ask, for ₹15,000? But her heart is left behind in an old crumbing villa …

Madhur gets up and unpacks her suitcases' contents into the cupboard. She opens the small refrigerator, absentmindedly, and sees that it's empty. 'I'll have to make my own food from now on,' she mutters to herself, and grabs her scooter keys, to go look for local stores. On the staircase she encounters Chaitali, who drags her across the road to her pink boutique.

Madhur is quite surprised at her collection. Chaitali makes asymmetrical dresses in earth colours, using organic fabrics like jute, linen, pure cotton and spun khadi. They are accessorized with jewellery made of dried flowers, twigs and leaves. Somehow, she expected to see pop-artish, bright and kitschy designs. 'Your collection is so muted …why is your shop so bright?' Madhur asks her.

'What to do? Earlier, I had a plain white structure with blue doors and windows. Nobody used to walk in. Now, people stop their cars and bikes, and enter,' she says.

'But are they the right kind of people?' Madhur asks, walking amongst the clothes racks, touching the fabric, checking the finish and the cuts.

'Haan, out of ten, only two will like and buy something. But they remember my shop as the pink shop and tell others about it.'

'*Haan, woh bhi sahi baat hain* (Yes, that is also right),' says Madhur, 'Chalo, I must go and stock up some groceries now.'

CHAPTER 19

Finders Keepers

Karl Mascarenhas gets a call from the Mapusa police station, one morning in the second week of December. It is PSI Shirsat, his classmate from school.

'Madhur Chopra works for you right?'

'Yes, as a freelancer, why do you ask?'

'I found her phone, a Vivo,' Shirsat says. 'So many lost and broken phones were retrieved from the Narkasur fiasco!'

'Oh great! I can take my old iPhone back from her,' Karl says delightedly. 'Shall I tell her to meet you at the station?'

'No wait! There's something else,' the PSI hesitates.

'What?'

'I can't tell you on phone. Meet me for a drink,' he says.

Karl's hackles are raised. 'Why Paresh?' he asks, 'I'm a bit busy… is it necessary to meet?'

'Arré baba, you just meet me, na. For old time's sake. Come alone, don't get the girl.'

Karl is worried by the call. What could possibly be the issue, he wonders. If the police find lost property—especially something like a phone—there are straightforward procedures for the owner to claim it. He decides to call Madhur. 'Hey, all well?' Karl asks, 'How's your new friend?'

'I'm fine, and so is Ms Enthu Cutlet,' she says laughing, 'What's up? Do you have some work for me?'

'Jacinta and I just wanted to invite you for drinks. Come over in the evening at 7, okay?'

'Cool.'

Jacinta opens the door, hugs Madhur and takes her inside. Karl is already drinking in the hall and watching Netflix. He switches it off on seeing her. Even though he's dressed in regular house clothes, he doesn't look relaxed. 'Come, come,' he says, 'Wine or Vodka?'

'Vodka with Sprite,' she says and plonks down on a sofa. Madhur can feel the tension in the air. She is certain that it has something to do with Stella. He hands her the drink and says, 'There's something I want to ask you.'

Madhur smiles knowingly.

'Just think carefully and tell me,' he says. 'Was there anything private on your lost phone?'

'My old phone? Did someone find it? Where?'

'A cop has it at Mapusa Police Station—and he's being very cagey about it.'

'What do you mean?' Madhur asks.

'I told him I'll get you to the station, and you'll fill the required forms, show your ID proof and take it back … but he wants to meet me alone. To discuss something over "drinks",' Karl says, making the air quote gesture.

'That's strange,' Madhur concurs. 'Why does he want to meet you when it's my phone?'

'Exactly! So, I'm asking you again—before I meet him—is there *anything* in your phone that you should worry about? Anything controversial or illegal? Anything that can be used against you?'

Madhur looks confused. 'No! It has videos and photos that are already online. There are some Narkasur videos that I didn't get to post, because we all ran and I dropped my phone.'

'So, nothing incriminating?'

'No!'

'Any private videos with boyfriends?'

'I don't have a boyfriend,' Madhur laughs.

'Girlfriends?'

'C'mon!'

'Okay then, I'll give that PSI Shirsat two tight slaps and bring your phone back tomorrow.'

CHAPTER 20

Cop-out

Madhur accepts her parcel from the Amazon delivery guy and runs inside her room to tear it open. The A3-sized, hand-made paper drawing book feels good to hold.

A couple of weeks prior, she finally decided to design clothes again. This was after being cajoled relentlessly by Chaitali, who dumped waste fabric from her boutique on Madhur, commissioning a new line of organic loungewear and beachwear. Chaitali had grudgingly agreed to keep three of Madhur's Madfashions outfits, even though they did not match her organic vibe. In return, she asked Madhur to do a new collection in organic fabrics.

'But why are you doing this for me, Chaitali?' Madhur had asked.

'Because I can, Madhur! I see so much creativity in you, and I want to help you get over your slump. You are a fashion designer from NIFT Delhi, no less! You shouldn't be doing graphic design work …'

'But *why* are you helping me?' Madhur had looked suspiciously at Chaitali.

'*Aai Saibini!* Why are you so suspicious? My god! You city folks! Just accept, na. I don't want anything in return, Madhur. I'm just being friendly, neighbourly—call it whatever you want.'

'Okay babaa, thank you!' Madhur had said, accepting the offer.

'Also, if I had not given up my NIFT seat, we would have been batchmates. And had we met in college, would you have been so suspicious of me now?'

Madhur didn't need to think much, she had smiled and hugged Chaitali in response. 'Yes, I would've definitely been your friend at NIFT. God knows I needed one desperately when I was there. And you, my dear, would have been the most popular girl in Delhi! The girl from Goa!'

Madhur can sketch on devices, but the feel of a lead pencil on paper is something else. Midway through her second practise sketch, her mobile rings with an unidentified caller.

'Is this Maddie—Madhur Chopra?'

'Yes, Madhur Chopra speaking.'

'Hi, please listen carefully,' says a squeaky voice.

'Who's speaking?'

'I think a cop is going to blackmail you, I'm just calling to warn you,' he says. In the background, Madhur can hear a lady screaming in Konkani, '*Jeoung yo! Soglo dis phonaar!* (Come to eat food! You're on your phone all day!)'

'Who's this? Is this a prank call? I'll call the police!' Madhur screams.

After a brief pause, he says, '*Abbey dhakkan!* (You dolt!) I'm warning you about cops and you want to go to them only?'

'*Par mainé kuch nahi kiya* (But I have not committed any crime), why should anybody blackmail me?' Madhur says, feeling frustrated.

'I'm a hacker,' he whispers, 'Mapusa police asked me to crack passwords of lost mobiles found during the Narkasur fire. It's the job of their cyber cell at Ribandar, but there are dinosaurs working there, so they bypassed those buggers and employed me.'

Madhur gets nervous. Yesterday Karl was acting all cagey, asking weird questions about her phone, and today a strange hacker is telling her that she might be blackmailed by police. '*Mera iss sé kya léna-déna?* (How does that involve me?)' she asks him.

'Did you lose a Vivo phone in the stampede?'

'*Arré yaar!* How can you be so sure it's mine?' Madhur is irritated now.

'Well, that's exactly why they pay me,' he replies, cockily.

'*Accha chalo, manlo ki méra hain* (Okay fine, lets presume that it belongs to me), so what? Let the police station contact me, and then I'll go collect it,' she says, trying to sound nonchalant.

'There's a PSI, who had used excuses like "Prevention of Terrorism Act" to make me look into people's online and offline data. The permission was granted, allegedly, with the purpose of finding out who or what started the fire.'

'My phone gallery has videos and photos that are already online,' she tells him.

'Hmm … I remember when he found out that it was your phone, he specifically asked me to look for unreleased videos of superstar Ricky Malhotra.'

Oh God, that name again! It always triggers memories she wants to forget. Forever.

'But there are none!' Madhur exclaims.

'There is! There is one that I found. And I'm sorry PSI Shirsat and I have watched it. I didn't realize that he was standing over my head when I found the video. I quickly put it under strong password protection. No one can crack it, except me. And I told him that file is corrupted now, and the video will not play again. Since then, he's been calling me every fifteen minutes, begging me to repair the video file.'

Madhur starts laughing, '*Mujhé chutiya banaa rahé ho kya?* (Are you trying to fool me?) There are no videos of Ricky Malhotra on my phone. I shot them on his iPhone. He then shared them with me, and I uploaded them all. *Kuch nahin milega!* (You'll find nothing!)'

'*Par milaa!*' he says, '*Bahut* private video *hain* (It's a very private video).'

'Impossible,' Madhur says, her heart thundering. How could it be possible? She thinks back to that dreaded afternoon. Her phone had fallen down somewhere in his car. Is it possible that … With a shaky voice she asks, 'I don't understand how the video exists in my phone … what to do now? Can you help me?'

'You should've erased your phone immediately after you lost it,' he reprimands her.

'I know, I forgot to do that. I was dealing with a personal tragedy, and by the time I remembered, the phone could not be located. I assumed that somebody switched it off or took out my sim card…'

'Has PSI Shirsat contacted you? He told me he will blackmail you on the basis of the video. He will threaten to release your video, even though he can't open it, and extort money from you to NOT release it.'

'He called my good friend, Karl Mascarenhas.'

'The event guy?'

'Yes, but PSI hasn't revealed anything, yet. He's asked Karl to meet him for drinks at 7.00 p.m. today.'

'Classic PSI Shirsat move.'

'So, what now?'

'Tell Karl Mascarenhas not to pay any money. I will access your phone remotely and wipe out all data. Then it will just be a dabba in PSI's hand.'

Madhur almost agrees to his suggestion, 'That would be great, but … I don't even know the video in question. I definitely didn't shoot it,' she says.

'Camera must've switched on by itself, due to some impact. It's shot from a low angle. The mobile was clearly on the floor.'

Suddenly, all the bells of Goa ring inside her head: church bells, temple bells … 'Shit, shit, shit,' Madhur says. 'Oh God, I must warn Karl. *Hey Ram, yeh kyun hua!* (Oh God! Why did this happen?)'

'Relax, Maddie. You're safe now. Nobody will see the video ever again,' he says.

'But you have! And that PSI too!'

'Haan … but he has not watched the entire video. And why should I watch you when there's Mia Khalifa,' he says, giggling. Madhur can't decide if she should be grateful to him or slap him.

'Okay, I'm going to call Karl now. Thank you—may I know your name?'

'Save my number in your contacts as "Hacker Shanx".'

'Okay, thanks, Shanx. I'll be in touch.'

She immediately gets on her scooter and rides to Karl's house. It's 6.00 p.m., and he's just returned from work, enjoying a cup of chai on his balcão. Madhur doesn't park her scooter, she lets it fall to the ground and jumps-off.

'Arré, arré, what happened?' he asks, looking worried.

Madhur runs to him and starts crying. Karl shepherds her inside the house, 'What happened, Maddie? Did Stella call and say something to you? Why you crying?'

Madhur can't stop bawling. Karl gestures to Jacinta for help. 'Okay, don't tell me. Would you like to tell Jacinta?'

Jacinta escorts Madhur from the hall to her bedroom and shuts the door. They stay inside and talk for half an hour. Karl starts pacing outside. 'Hey guys, how much longer? Remember, I have to meet Shirsat at 7.00 …'

On hearing the name, Madhur starts crying again. Jacinta opens the door, with a pensive look on her face, she says, 'Don't meet Shirsat, there's been some new development.'

'Huh?'

Looking at Madhur, Jacinta says, 'Maddie, you tell him. He's like your big brother.'

'What's going on, Jacinta? Is she in trouble? Has that bastard Shirsat called her?'

'No, no, wait. Let Maddie tell you,' Jacinta tells her impatient and infuriated husband.

In between sobbing and sniffling, Madhur tells Karl everything. Right from the meeting with Ricky Malhotra, followed by the assault in the superstar's car, to the recent Hacker Shanx' call. Karl's eyes are bulging out by the time she's done narrating her story. 'So, you're telling me,' he says, 'that the bloody PSI is going to pull a bluff on me?'

'That's what Hacker Shanx said.'

'Are you sure that Shirsat doesn't know how to access that video? What if he gets another hacker to crack Shanx's password?'

'Hmmm, it's possible ...' Madhur says, tearing up again.

'Arré, you stop crying, men! What's done is done. Can you change it?'

'Easy for you to say ... I'll have to kill myself if that video leaks out.'

'Maddie! Kill the video first. Tell Shanx to erase it. I'll pay him.'

Jacinta interrupts, 'What if they're in this together? Playing Bad Cop–Good Hacker?'

'Point!' exclaims Karl. Madhur starts bawling again.

'Is the hacker really willing to help? Can he be trusted?' Jacinta asks Madhur.

'He seemed genuine, plus he sounded like a kid and not like a hardened criminal.'

'Then we have to have faith,' Karl says to Madhur. 'Here's the plan, I'll meet Shirsat at 7.00—damn, it's already 7.30. Maddie, you meet the hacker kid right now. Get him to erase the phone remotely-shimotely, whatever shit they do, while I engage PSI in talk.'

'My phone has to be switched on for the hacker to gain access—it's important.' she says.

'Okay, I'll ensure that.'

CHAPTER 21

The Hack Job

Madhur calls Hacker Shanx and requests to see him immediately. He agrees to meet at Arbor in Saligão—a micro-brewery restaurant that's always empty, so no one will overhear their conversation. Madhur wonders if he's below legal drinking age, as she listens to him talk excitedly about flavoured beer. A quick Google survey reveals that she cannot afford any drink there. Hacker Shanx immediately offers to treat her. Now, Madhur's hackles are raised.

She arrives at the bar by 8.00 p.m. and waits for Shanx. He's right about the place—it has more waiters than people, making it a perfect choice for their rendezvous. It's an al-fresco garden bar, with a tarpaulin canopy. The bar counter has wood-panelling, with barrels of beer placed on top. Dim lighting gives the place a smoky, cabin-in-the-woods feel.

Across the street from the bar, there's a stately chapel and some lovely old houses, reminding her of Casa Coutinho. It's been a month since she moved out, and not a day passes when she doesn't think of something or the other related to her time there. Madhur busies herself by studying the menu, when suddenly she hears a commotion outside. She stands up and sees a traffic jam, to her surprise, with car and bike owners honking with urgency. It's a very small, nondescript village road to merit such a thing, and Madhur hopes it's not an accident. As vehicles slowly snake around an unseen obstruction and clear the road, she hears some teenagers laughing and talking loudly. They have parked their rented bikes haphazardly beside a white villa and are taking selfies. Madhur's curiosity is piqued, and she walks closer to the Arbor compound wall to investigate. The white villa has an interesting mural painted on its wall. The teenagers pose with obscene gestures beside a mural of a priest or an abbot, skilfully rendered with spray paint.

Madhur glares at them from across the narrow street. Unfortunately, she makes eye contact with a young girl in the group. The girl freezes for a second, as if she's just seen a ghost. Eyes still transfixed on Madhur, she whispers something into her partner's ear. Now, the group of six confer amongst themselves for a few seconds. Madhur knows what's going to happen next and she grits her teeth in anticipation. The girl crosses the narrow street and shouts, 'Maddie? Maddie Chopra?'

'Haan.'

'Why aren't you vlogging anymore? I came to Goa because of "Maddie Vlogs from Goa",' she tells Madhur.

She points at them and explodes, 'That's why! *Ek toh yeh itni chotisi street hai, uspé aap traffic jam kavra rahein ho, apni harkaton sé!* (It's a such a narrow street to begin with, and you are all causing a traffic jam with your antics!) You should come early morning to take pictures—the light is better and you won't be disturbing the locals going about their daily lives! What's the point of taking selfies in this streetlamp light?'

Somebody says, '*Tu buddhi hogayi hain!* (You've become old!)' and they all snigger. An enraged Madhur is about to spew venom, but she is stopped by a tap on her shoulder.

A tall, lanky guy is towering over her. Madhur looks up questioningly at the fellow dressed in a loose black hoodie over red, skin-tight jeans. His face is covered with an N95 black mask, and he is wearing sunglasses at night. How easy it is to hide one's identity in these times, she muses.

'Hi Maddie,' he says in his squeaky voice.

'Shanx?'

'Yup, shall we?' he says and walks inside to the seating area. Pulling a chair, he looks at a waiter and says, 'The usual.'

Clearly, he is a regular here, thinks Madhur, still standing.

'Oh hey, please sit,' he says, and pulls out two laptops from his backpack. 'Order whatever you like, but like I said—'

'The beers are the best. I know, but I'll have a coffee though.'

Madhur sits and waits. Hacker Shanx takes off his sunglasses and smiles shyly at her, crinkling his warm brown eyes. He starts setting up his laptops and other gadgets. Meanwhile, the waiter gets his beer and Madhur's coffee. 'I will erase your phone in front of you,' he says, 'so you have proof that I did it.'

'And …' she hesitates, '… how much will you charge?'

'Nothing. Okay, not nothing. I have a small favour to ask of you,' he says, with puppy-dog eyes.

Madhur is not amused. She thinks the worst, spying a hormonal teenager behind the mask. 'What favour? Wait! *Shurru mat kario!* (Don't you start!)'

'Please hear me out! I have a tech vlog and a podcast. All I am asking is you appear on both. It's a simple barter deal. No complex or hidden terms and conditions. Cool with you?' he asks, while furiously tapping the keyboards.

Madhur bursts out laughing. She reaches across the table and grabs his cheeks underneath his facemask with her hands, much to his embarrassment. 'Yes, *mere bacche* (my child)!' she says, feeling relieved for the first time in two days. '*Par tu mujhe ek baat bataa* (But tell me one thing), why are you helping me? Is this some kind of trap?'

'No trap, God-promise,' he says, pinching his prominent Adam's apple. 'I only use my skills for good. We're both digital age people, so we must have each other's back. We must not allow the analog dinosaurs to be the gate keepers of OUR digital era. Given a chance, they'll sabotage internet freedom. They'll survey every app on every device, by using "safety" as an excuse, when in reality they're just getting their kicks watching us at our most vulnerable and private moments,' he finishes, trying to catch his breath.

Madhur does a fist and says, 'Jai mata di! *Bahut kuch bol dia, par sahi bol dia!* (You said a lot, but said the right thing!)'

'So, *shurru karein*? Come, sit by my side,' he says. 'Okay, message sent. PSI will click on the link, and then I will gain access.'

'If he doesn't click on your link, then?'

'He will click. I am sure, because of my message.'

'What message?'

'"Corrupt Video files? Don't lose your favourite video memories. Click to download free video repair software. Easy to use; get first five video repair free!'

Madhur is gobsmacked, 'O my god, Shanx! You *Jamtara*[5] people ... do your parents know?'

'First of all, I don't *Jamtara* people. I have ethics. And I learnt from the best—my dad,' he says. Glancing at his laptops, he gestures to stop talking. Has the PSI clicked on the link? They are at the edge of their seats. Shanx sips his beer, as soundlessly as possible, staring at both his laptops. Madhur stares at him. After ten minutes, he exclaims, 'I'm in! Works all the time!' He hi-fives Madhur and turns the screens towards her. 'See, here are all your folders. Do you want to save anything?' Madhur looks at his laptop screen, but it's all in code. 'I can't read this! It could be anything! *Tu mujhey Matrix kay number dikha raha hain, main kyun maan lu ki woh méré files hain?* (You are showing me Matrix-like numbers, and expect me to believe that these are my phone's folders?)'

'Ai Saiba,' he says, exasperated. 'I'll download them to my desktop, okay? I was avoiding that, because then you can accuse me of saving copies of your files.'

'I won't.'

'There, I've erased your phone now. PSI will not know what hit him!'

'May I see my files?' she asks. He nods and excuses himself for a smoke.

Madhur watches all her old videos and becomes emotional. She is grateful that Shanx saved a back-up. There are ten videos of Mrs Coutinho at the Narkasur parade, smiling deliriously; Madhur's last happy memories of Aunty before she suffered the

---

5 Reference to a Netflix series in Hindi about small town mobile hackers in India.

stroke. Scrolling further, she finds the contentious video. She picks up the laptop and walks away, to stand with her back against a wall at the far end of the garden. Muting the sound, she watches it carefully.

Superstar Ricky Malhotra's face is clearly visible throughout the video. Her face is visible for a few seconds only, and then her hair covers it. The video must go, she resolves, keeping the rising bile down in her throat. Shanx comes back and stands by her side, maintaining sufficient distance between them. He reaches out and offers her his cigarette. She takes a long drag. '*Sirf yeh video delete karo* (Delete this video), and give me the rest,' she says, handing him a pen drive.

'Thank you, Shanx. I owe you,' she says. He gives her a sideways hug, settles the bill, packs his tech paraphernalia, and they both walk to the parking lot. Climbing astride a Red Harley, he zooms away shattering the stillness of the night. Madhur looks on, 'Stud saala! Harley-Sharley *chalata hain*!' she says aloud, smiling fondly. She takes out her mobile and messages Karl, 'It's done.'

Karl reads the message and smiles. He orders two more bottles of beer, ignoring PSI Shirsat's protests. 'Maar marré,' Karl says, 'duty over, no?'

'So?' PSI Shirsat asks, drunkenly. 'It's not much for a big man like you. She's your employee, no?'

'Freelancer,' Karl corrects him. 'And she's just twenty-four, a child, ya …'

'Not my child, no! She may be a child for you,' PSI says curtly, trying to get a rise out of Karl, who has no children after more than twenty years of marriage.

'Don't be like that, Paresh. She is somebody's child na? And by the way, money's not a problem, but *shaanya*, we've been yapping and drinking for two hours now, you've not shown me any video or phone,' Karl says. In response, Shirsat waves the phone at him, 'Here it is! Good phone, but it's not iPhone.'

'Show me the video now,' Karl repeats. 'Then I'll take you to an ATM right away, withdraw cash and give you.'

'Let's go out then,' PSI suggests. Karl settles the bill and they step out of Satyaheera Restaurant, near Shivaji Circle. Once they are outside, the cop starts scrolling through Madhur's phone. Suddenly he scratches his head and looks confused. 'Wait, it's hung. Let me try restarting it,' he says.

It's 10.00 p.m. and the traffic in Mapusa is thinning down steadily. Karl walks away from PSI Shirsat to the footpath opposite the restaurant. He stands outside the Ram Manohar Lohiya Municipal Garden, where they had sought refuge during the Narkasur fiasco. Remembering the painful night, he turns to look in the direction of the Maruti temple, and mumbles 'thank you'.

PSI Shirsat, meanwhile, is engrossed in a call with someone, staring at Madhur's phone in his hand. Karl walks to a small cigarette stand and buys a pack. He quit smoking many years ago, but if he doesn't keep his hands busy, he's afraid he'll wrap them around Shirsat's neck and strangle him to death. After two minutes, he stomps over the cigarette butt and walks purposefully towards the PSI.

'*Kidhém jaalé?* (What's going on?)' Karl asks him, 'Do you want money or not?'

'*Deo zannam ré* (God knows), one minute the video was here, and now it's gone.'

'*Mojhi firki ghetaam ré!* (Are you trying to trick me?)' Karl says sarcastically.

The PSI is apologetic, '*Na ré? Firki kid'yaank gheoum?* (No man, why will I try to trick you?) I only must have deleted it by mistake. Here, take the phone,' he says handing the phone to Karl.

Karl puts ₹5,000 in the PSI's shirt pocket and walks to his parked car. He calls Madhur from inside his car.

'I have your phone,' he says excitedly, 'you better return mine first thing tomorrow.'

'I'm already waiting at your house with it,' Madhur replies.

CHAPTER 22

Fashionistas Conquistas

Chaitali barges into Madhur's room one evening, breathless and excited. 'I want to participate in Fashion Week '22,' she announces. 'It's being held in Delhi, sometime in the month of November.'

'Okay,' says Madhur, 'it's still March, *kaam shurru kar* (start working).'

'I need your help,' Chaitali says nervously.

'Babe, you know I prefer pastel shades and non-organic fabrics. I can't be all Earth-mother-goddess like you. I tried, but I'm no good.'

'No, no, I just need you to model my creations, style them, take pictures and write me a reference letter,' she says in a rush. 'I'll pay you.'

'Modelling, styling and photography *theek hain, par méra* reference *ka koi mainé nahi hain* (okay, but my reference will not have any value). Get a well-known personality to give you that,' Madhur advises.

'But you are a well-known personality—a famous fashion blogger from Delhi!'

Madhur laughs, '*Woh sirf video mein bolné ké liye hain.* (That is only for videos.)'

Chaitali looks deflated. Madhur feels sorry for her, '*Accha chal* (okay), I'll help you with the work you mentioned. I'll assist you in creating a portfolio of your work too. *Naam socha* fashion line *ka?* (Have you thought of a name for you fashion line?)'

'*Sochney ki kya zaroorat hain?* (Why do I need to think of one?) It will be "Chaitali"!' she says triumphantly.

Madhur looks bewildered. '*Paagal hain?* No! It won't work,' she scolds Chaitali, 'It's okay for your shop, but this is Fashion Week you're talking about.'

'So you tell, na,' says Chaitali.

'Please don't feel bad, but "Chaitali" sounds like a photocopier shop in Paharganj. Think of a name with Portuguese roots, like "Por Favor", "Obrigado", "Bom dia" … Open Google Translate and translate whatever name you are thinking of to Portuguese language.'

'First of all, where's Paharganj? And those Portuguese words you're throwing about—they mean "Please", "Thank you" and "Good Day". They'll sound so stupid for a fashion brand!'

'Chaitali! Only you know their meanings—not the Mumbai-Delhi aunties who attend Fashion Week! *Tu meri baat sunn liya kar yaar!* (Listen to what I have to say!)'

'I don't agree,' Chaitali says petulantly.

'Fine, *tera* surname *kya hain* (what's your surname)? Haanjookar?'

'Hanjunkar,' Chaitali corrects her pronunciation.

'*Matlab?* Your family is from Haanjun? Where's that? In China?'

Chaitali rolls her eyes, '"Anjuna" is called "Hanjuna" in Konkani. Some people spell it as "Anjunkar", but we prefer "Hanjunkar"—it's the same thing though.'

Madhur's eyes light up. She puts her laptop away, stands up on her bed and does a little dance, singing, 'Anjuna! Anjuna! Boom Shaka Laka Anjuna!'

Chaitali starts laughing, 'Had a smoke awhat?'

Madhur gives her a hi-five, 'Call it "Anjuna", and make it out of hemp fabric! Use the hemp leaf motif to accessorize!'

Chaitali gets excited and climbs up on the bed too. They both hold hands and start jumping and screaming 'Anjuna, Anjuna, Boom Shaka Laka Anjuna! Anjuna, Anjuna, Boom Shaka Laka Anjuna!'

Madhur's phone starts ringing, interrupting their celebration. It's Karl. She picks it up and gestures to Chaitali to lower her volume.

'Party-sharty *ho raha hain* (happening)? he asks, mimicking her Delhi accent.

'No, no, Chaitali and I just had a creative breakthrough,' she replies. 'Tell me?'

'Our good friend Stella is here and she wants to meet you.'

'*Kyun?* I'm no longer living in Casa Coutinho,' Madhur says in a raised tone, her mood souring in seconds. Sensing the change in mood, Chaitali excuses herself and leaves the room.

'She wants to thank you. Just meet her for two minutes only,' Karl urges Madhur.

'Tell her to thank me on phone.'

'She's got lots of chocolates for you, come yaar! For two minutes only.'

'*Abhi?*' she asks.

'Yes, abhi.'

Madhur changes into formal clothes and leaves for Karl's house. She meets Chaitali on the staircase. 'I'll be back in half an hour, and then we'll work through the night, okay?' she tells her.

Ten minutes later, Madhur parks outside Karl's house. She hears a heated exchange in Konkani, coming from the house. It is so loud, it can be heard on the street. Unsure of whether to knock, she sits in the balcão and waits, wondering why she bothered coming at all. After a few minutes, she gets up and strolls into the compound to play with a stray dog who's always around. The door swings open all of a sudden, and a smartly dressed, heavily perfumed, middle-aged lady storms out of the house towards the entrance gate. She makes eye contact with Madhur, stops for a second in her tracks, then looks away haughtily towards a private taxi parked outside. Madhur continues petting the dog, pretending not to see or care. After the taxi zooms off, Jacinta comes out of the door. She spots Madhur and says, 'Oh, you are here! Why didn't you come inside?'

'I heard some screaming, so I thought it would be better to wait outside.'

Jacinta bursts out laughing. 'Come, come, the dramas in our house never end,' she says. Once inside, she introduces Madhur to an old gentleman with silver hair, having drinks and chatting with Karl. 'Shirodkar Uncle, this is Madhur Chopra. I was telling you about her, remember?'

The old gentleman gets up and shakes her hand. 'Nice to meet you, Madhur! You're prettier than Jacinta described you,' he says, eyes twinkling. Madhur blushes and sits down.

Karl smiles at her and asks, 'Maddie, do you want to run an NGO?'

Taken aback by the sudden offer, she replies hastily, 'What? No chance! I'm not the Jhola-Kolhapuri chappal type.'

'Cheh, Cheh! Don't scare her like that, Karl. *Borya bashein* explain *kar marré*. (Explain it to her properly.)' Shirodkar Uncle says and gets up to leave. Turning to Madhur, he says, 'I'll see you around, young lady. You young folks enjoy your evening.'

Karl and Jacinta escort him out to the gate. They continue talking animatedly for five more minutes, till a white Mercedes Benz 1970s' model comes and whisks the old man away.

The couple enter their house with a smile, plonk themselves on the sofa on either side of Madhur and hug her. Karl lets out a huge sigh and says, 'Finally!'

He looks at her and asks, 'What was it you were singing when I called? Sajana, Sajana, gale lagja Sajna?'

'No! "Anjuna, Anjuna, Boom Shaka Laka Anjuna!"' Madhur laughs uncontrollably as Karl rolls his eyes. He goes to his drinks cabinet and pulls out a bottle of Absolut. 'No Boom Shaka Laka here, but I can give you my best vodka,' he says, fixing a drink for her.

'No Karl! I have to go back. I promised Chaitali that I'd return in thirty minutes,' she says and stands up to leave.

'Wait! I have to tell you what happened!'

Madhur hesitates, 'Karl, it's your family matter …'

'Didn't you hear what Shirodkar Uncle said? It's important for you to listen.'

Madhur looks concerned now.

Karl smiles deliriously, 'First, ask me why I'm so happy?' he urges Madhur.

'Why are you so happy, Karl? Tell me quick, I have to leave!'

'Because our friend Stella just got her arse bitten by karma! Casa Coutinho cannot be sold! And I'm so happy, even though I'm losing my 2 per cent cut!' he declares.

'Okay,' says Madhur, sounding uncertain.

'Uncle Godfrey had left a will behind, and Shirodkar Uncle is its executor. The will comes into force now, after Aunty Mabel's death,' Karl continues. 'But the biggest revelation today, for me and Jacinta, was that Stella has an older sister,' Karl says taking a sip of the drink he had fixed for Madhur. Jacinta pulls Madhur's hand and makes her sit on the sofa. 'Stella knew about her sibling! It's their family secret, and she never mentioned it!' he exclaims.

Still feeling uncertain about her role in the family drama, Madhur stands up to leave, '*Chalo accha hua* (It's great then), the older sister will look after the house now.'

'Arré wait! Hear the whole story. It involves you too! Sit!' he commands.

'The older sister is mentally retarded. She's in a home for special people in Thivim right now, run by the Sisters of Compassion. She's been there since her birth.'

Looking at Jacinta he says, 'I can't believe Uncle Godfrey, Aunty Mabel and, even, Stella kept this a secret for so long. So, all those trips to a Thivim Orphanage meant that she was visiting her older daughter, and not for charity work as she claimed. Oh my God!'

'Karl, dear, you're conveniently forgetting that it happened in the early 1970s. It was a different time back then. Mental illness was the biggest taboo, to have an intellectually challenged child was considered a curse and bad luck for the family. It's quite possible that the Coutinhos told everybody that their first child died at birth,' Jacinta explains to Karl, 'And don't say "mentally retarded"—the child is autistic,' she scolds Karl.

He continues, ignoring his wife's scolding, 'According to the will, Angela, the autistic, older child—what "child", she's in her fifties now—is an equal share holder in the house. Uncle Godfrey was aware that Stella had no interest in coming back to Goa, so he put a "No Sale" clause. Stella is most welcome to stay in the house, if she leaves the UK and comes back. She doesn't even have to take care of the older sibling. Angela will remain with the Sisters of Compassion, and the parents have made financial provisions for that too. But, if Stella chooses to stay in the UK, then the house goes to the Sisters of Compassion. Casa Coutinho will soon be an institution for intellectually challenged girls and women.'

'Wow!' Madhur says, still reeling from the shocking revelation.

Jacinta smiles, 'It completely blew my mind. Sounds like a Hindi film story, men!'

'So, Maddie, would you like to go back to Casa Coutinho, only this time as an administrator of this noble institution?'

'Me? I know nothing about mental health or its related issues,' Madhur exclaims.

'The job is only for supervision,' explains Karl. 'Shirodkar Uncle said that ideally some family member should be associated with the home, as it still belongs to the Coutinhos. But since Stella disowned her entire family, the responsibility and a place in its administrative board falls on me. But as you know, I'm busy with my events and would not trade that for anything. So, I, Karl Mascarenhas, nominate you, Madhur Chopra in my place. I know you love the house, and this way you'll get your room back. You can earn a salary, with no rent to pay. You'll have help from all the nuns and ladies around. You can do so much good for society,' he says delightedly. 'So, what do you say?'

Madhur looks at the time on her mobile, 'No, thank you, you only do it. I'm happy with where I am.'

'*Tu araam se socchle* (Take your time to consider it), no rush,' says Karl.

'My answer will still be "no",' Madhur says.

Karl looks disappointed.

'Karl, I don't doubt your intentions. I can see why you think I'd be a good fit for the role, but ... I can't see myself doing social service. In fact, I'm getting back to fashion design ... I cannot do this. Not now. I'm sorry,' Madhur says and bids them goodnight.

Her mind is boggled by the sudden turn of events. All these Goan families and their complicated ancestries, interspersed with sibling rivalries. She wants none of it. Casa Coutinho was close to her heart because of Aunty Coutinho. But without her, it's just any other old Goan villa.

Madhur rides fast to Shubhangi Niwas. She is happy there, her life is less complicated now, sprinkled with the occasional 'Anjuna! Anjuna!' to gladden her heart. All said and done, Chaitali's behaviour still bothers her. Chaitali is an upright kid with a good upbringing—a bit like her—individualistic, yet conservative. Maybe that's the reason why she is irritated by her—Chaitali reminds Madhur of herself from five years ago, before the world broke her down.

While climbing the stairs to her apartment, she bumps into Chaitali, 'Aye, don't you have a room? *Tu seediyon pe hi rehti hain?* (Do you live on these stairs?)'

'*Tera wait kar rahi thi* (I was waiting for you),' Chaitali mumbles sullenly, 'It's 10.00 p.m. already.'

'*Meri maa!* The night is still young! I'll go eat some dinner, and then we'll work. It'll take ten minutes, okay? Come, sit in my room,' Madhur pulls her along.

After a quick bite, Madhur settles down on her bed with Chaitali. It's just big enough for the two petite girls to lie side by side on their backs.

'The procedure to apply for Fashion Week is a bit complicated, especially for the new designers,' says Chaitali. 'First, I need to apply for membership to the Fashion Council.'

'*Haan ... toh kar na! Chal,* sketches *banaatey hain!* (Yes ... so do it! Let's make some sketches now!)' Madhur says, jumping out of the bed. She throws a sketch pad at Chaitali, takes one for herself and squats on the floor. 'Here is pencil, pen, sketch pen—choose whatever you prefer.'

Midway through their sketching task, Madhur's phone starts pinging continuously. She ignores it and continues with her work. After two minutes of the constant pinging, Chaitali looks irritated and begs her to check it. Madhur is afraid it'll be Karl or Jacinta. Then the phone rings. 'Oh my god! Who's calling at midnight? Got a boyfriend awhat?' Chaitali asks, raising her eyebrows.

It's Hacker Shanx. Madhur takes a deep breath before answering.

'Hello,' she says. '*Kya hua?*'

'Nothing ... just called to remind you of your promise,' he says.

'What promise ...Oh! Of course, I haven't forgotten. When do you want to do it?'

'Tomorrow?' he asks.

'Next week? I'm busy working on a project right now,' Madhur says.

He agrees and Madhur bids him good night. She returns to her sketch pad on the floor.

Chaitali looks at her and smiles. Madhur frowns at the unsaid implications.

'*Koi boyfriend-voyfriend nahin hain* (He is not my boyfriend). He's just a vlogger kid and a techy influencer. He has invited me to talk on his podcast.'

'Nice!' Chaitali exclaims, 'So it's like a vlogger collab—fashion meets tech.'

'*Koi collab nahin.* (It's not a collab.) I'm not vlogging anymore. He helped me with something, so I'm returning the favour. I'll share some photography and video tips on his channels ... bas!'

CHAPTER 23

Blog-Vlog

Madhur stops near the Milagres Church in Mapusa. There are three roads going in three different directions. Which one goes to Gaunsa vaddo? She checks her Google Maps again and proceeds straight down a narrow lane on her left. Riding slowly, she searches for Prabhavati Mansion. Shanx has asked her to look out for a maroon-coloured house. It's pinned as 'Shanx's Dungeon' on Google Maps, much to the chagrin of his parents.

Madhur recognizes a red bike parked inside a compound. The compound has a messy, overgrown garden. The maroon house is at least fifty metres away, almost hidden by the surrounding foliage. She parks her scooter beside the bike and walks towards the house. Out of nowhere, three Rottweilers come bounding towards her, barking like crazy. She hears a lady scream from inside the house, 'Shankar! Tie those damn dogs! They'll kill somebody!' Madhur freezes. The dogs sniff around her ankles and sit in a circle around her, looking up at her. Just then Shanx comes flying through the open door, with three leads in his hand. Seeing the dogs seated obediently, he stops and says, 'Nice! You're not afraid of them.'

Madhur looks at him and starts laughing, 'Your name is Shankar!'

He looks embarrassed, 'Only my mom calls me that.'

He leashes his dogs and drags them inside the house, with Madhur following. An ornately carved nameplate announces 'The Sardessais'. He takes Madhur to his recording studio.

It's a small compact set up at the corner of his large room. One area has a DSLR camera on a tripod for shooting vlogs, complete with a green screen backdrop for adding post-production graphics. The podcast area has two comfortable chairs, with a Shure Mic, Yamaha mixers and two noise-cancelling Sennheiser headphones. Madhur is envious and recognizes that the boy is from a rich family.

On the other side of his room—under his bed, over the study table, on top of his wardrobe—there are stacks upon stacks of brown cartons of different sizes.

She points to them and asks, 'Amazon addiction?'

'Free tech products from various companies, for trial and review.'

'Wah! *Tumsé koi sikhein!* (People should learn from you!)' she says. 'You are the OG influencer.'

Shanx positions her against the green backdrop, 'We'll record the podcast and vlog simultaneously,' he says, shifting mics and recorders closer. 'I don't do live shows. I prefer to edit,' he adds. 'You prefer going live, na?'

'Used to,' she says nonchalantly. 'Not anymore …'

She opens his channel on her phone. 'I checked your channel before coming here,' she says. 'I can't believe you started in 2008! How old are you now?'

'Twenty-two,' he answers.

Madhur raises an eyebrow, 'So, you started vlogging when you were eight years old? I thought I was a champion for starting at twelve.'

'Then you better not ask me when I hacked my first computer!' he says and laughs in his usual, irritating manner. Madhur wishes he could use Voice Changer in real life, just like he uses to sound mature and have a deeper baritone in his podcasts and videos.

Shanx explains the podcast theme to Madhur. 'We're going to talk about safe-guarding personal information on lost devices. In the first two minutes, I'll introduce you, talk about your erstwhile social media pages. After a brief introduction of your work, I'll start the Q&A session,' he says, adjusting her mic stand and sound controls.

'Shanx,' she says, concern in her voice. 'I read the questions you mailed me. I'm okay with most, but I don't want to mention PSI Shirsat. I'll get into trouble for it.' And after a pause, she adds, 'And so will you!'

'Me? No!' he says. Madhur looks up and sees that he's wearing sunglasses and a red facemask with the words 'Hacker Shanx' spray painted in white.

She stands up angrily, almost toppling the mic stand—holding it in the nick of time. 'Oh! You get to wear a mask to hide your identity, but I have to sit here, bare faced, answering all these incriminating questions? Is it fine to expose me? *Kaisey aadmi ho tum, yaar?* (What kind of a man are you?)'

'Okay, okay,' he quickly concedes. 'Let's cancel that question. We can talk casually about how you lost your phone—don't mention the Narkasur fire, if you don't want to.

After pausing and waiting for Madhur to calm down, 'You can talk about how I helped you trace your phone and erase it. Then I will explain the step-by-step process of how people can erase their data using "Find My Device",' he says to her.

'Okay, fine,' she says and sits down. 'And also cancel the superstar Ricky Malhotra question.'

'Why? I'm not referring to *that* video … it's about the reel you made, just before he died. It happens to be his last video. Do you know how many news channels shared it on their sites? It got millions of views. And like an idiot you went offline, deactivating all your accounts. You could've made so much money! You still can, if you get a good lawyer,' he says.

Ricky Malhotra is dead, just let him be.'

'I should have done this podcast by myself, what's the point of calling a celebrity vlogger?'

'I am not a celebrity, but I have every right to decline answering some of your questions. It's my trauma, and I do not want to talk about it. Do we agree? Shanx?'

'Yes … sorry.'

 *After a quick sound check, they begin shooting, and chat animatedly for half an hour. As Shanx finishes explaining the procedure to erase data, Madhur interrupts.*

MADHUR: And please do this immediately, the second you realize your phone is lost.

SHANX: That is a very important point to remember. Thank you for mentioning it, Maddie. But you didn't erase your missing phone immediately. Why didn't you do it?

MADHUR: I already told you.

SHANX: Yes, but tell it to our viewers and listeners.

MADHUR: I wish I had the benefit of listening to a podcast like this before my phone went missing. All you guys are so lucky. Thank you, Shanx.

SHANX: Thank you for your compliment!

MADHUR: Honestly, the night I lost my phone, I was concerned about it for a brief period of time. But I had a personal emergency. My missing phone was the last thing on my mind, because a loved one had a stroke and she died later ... so ... But I realize the importance of erasing my phone data immediately via this app ...

SHANX: Yes, data thieves will be able to access your email, your banking details, your photo gallery…

He pauses to check her reaction.

SHANX: There's a narrow window of time for you to take action, before the data is leaked … the misuse and abuse of your data can be endless, and quite scary.

MADHUR: Yes, yes. (*pause*) Sorry, but I must say something else.

SHANX: Yes?

MADHUR: I want to emphasize to all of you that data is powerful. Your data in someone else's hand can become a weapon. Bad people are always looking for ways to become powerful. You may never know their true intentions till the last minute … so stay alert and stay safe.

SHANX: And that's all folks! Stay wild, stay fearless! This is Hacker Shanx with Maddie Chopra of "Maddie Vlogs from Goa" and Madfashions, signing out! See ya soon!

MADHUR: Like and subscribe to this channel. Link is down below. You can listen to Hacker Shanx on Spotify too!

As he walks her out of his house, she stops briefly to admire his Harley.

'Want to take it for a ride?' he asks her.

'No way! My scooter is best.'

'Maddie,' he says hesitantly, 'I'm sorry for what happened to you ... but you must talk about it. In fact, I believe that you should activate all your social media accounts and let people know the truth about Ricky Malhotra. So what if he's dead? All his fans should know what a bastard he was. God knows how many more women he had abused. Maybe they will find strength to come out with their stories ...'

'*Kya farak padega?* (How will it help?) Will it stop another abuser?' she asks, sitting astride her scooter and fastening her helmet. 'It will reflect badly on me only. His fans will never accept the truth and will try to diss me. They will dissect each and every part of my life and tear me to shreds. What if they come after me in Goa? Threaten me with death or some other harm? I live alone, you know. What if they find out that my mother is a widow and also lives alone, and threaten to harm her? What if they come in groups to gangrape me? Haan? *Phir kya? Tu bachaayega mujhey? Ya* PSI Shirsat? *Kucch bhi mat bol!* (Then what? Will you rescue me? Or PSI Shirsat? Think before you speak!) It's not easy for female influencers. Women are second class citizens in the social media space also, just as in life.'

'At least consider going to therapy, Madhur. You were sexually abused—'

'Shut up!' she says, 'therapy-verapy, *yeh sab badey logon ké shauk hain* (are hobbies of the rich). People like me have to just suck it up and move on,' she says and rides off.

CHAPTER 24

Straightjacketed Angel

Madhur and Chaitali are busy procuring hemp fabric. They get samples from a big manufacturer in Mumbai and some smaller ones in Goa. One of the requirements for debutant designers at the Fashion Week is that they have to associate with a cause. A weavers' association, an NGO, or a women's collective.

'Instead of cloth, let's buy hemp fibre, and ask the kunbi weavers to weave it into fabric,' Chaitali suggests.

They not only have to choose between the different varieties of hemp available in the market, they need to find a reliable source for the material at a reasonable rate too. Moreover, they are yet to decide what cause they will support. Will Karl be able to help, Madhur wonders.

Madhur rides to Karl and Jacinta's place. Reaching their house, she sees that the couple is dressed to go out. 'I should've called,' Madhur says apologetically, 'I just took a chance. I'll come again tomorrow, to discuss something regarding our Fashion Week project.'

'Wait Madhur! Why don't you join us? We're going to visit the Sisters of Compassion Home, and after that we're having lunch at Spice Goa—you'll love their fish thaali,' Jacinta says.

'Let's discuss your project along the way.' Karl offers.

Madhur smiles, 'Jacinta, you had me at fish thaali!'

As they drive on the NH 66 highway, Madhur briefs Karl on the Fashion Week requirements. He listens patiently and then calls his accounts executive, instructing him to speak to all the NGOs in Goa, to see who'll be willing to work with Madhur and Chaitali. 'Don't worry,' he tells her, 'by tomorrow it will be sorted. You girls pay attention to designing.'

The Sisters of Compassion Home is in the middle of the bustling Thivim town, only a ten minutes' walk from the Thivim railway station. Some kind soul had donated their old ancestral house to the Sisters, similar to what the late Coutinho couple had planned for their own house. Shirodkar Uncle arrives ten minutes after them. Karl and Jacinta are here as witnesses to the MOU being signed between the Sisters and the Coutinho Estate executor. Madhur has just tagged along.

While the elders are handling legalities, Madhur wanders outside into the backyard. Several young girls and a few old women are tending to a garden. They are dressed in white, oversized men's shirts, worn over their saris and frocks, with either hats or towels covering their heads 'Shouldn't have worn a black turtleneck top,' she mutters and quickly runs to stand under a mango tree. 'My god, March *khatam hua nahin*, May *mein kya hoga?* (March isn't over yet, what will happen by May?)' she whispers, looking up. The temperature in the shade is four to five degrees cooler.

The back garden opens out into a vast tract of fields. Small patches of land are demarcated with a green mesh fabric, each patch growing a different vegetable, like okra, tomato, cabbage, cauliflower and bottle gourd. A toothless old woman gets up from her haunches and offers Madhur a cauliflower. Madhur refuses it, and points to the lauki patch instead. The old woman hollers at a young girl tending to the lauki patch. She picks up the biggest one and gives it to Madhur.

The residents are used to visitors and tourists. They always put on their best behaviour, in the hope of attracting sizeable donations. As Madhur walks around, cradling her huge bottle gourd, a young sister comes running towards her. 'Take it only if you're going to eat it,' she tells Madhur. 'That old lady keeps foisting vegetables on visitors and villagers. Just to stop us from selling the surplus.'

'I'll eat it,' she informs the disappointed sister. 'Apart from farming, what else do these women do?' Madhur asks, indulging the young sister in small talk. The sister agrees to show her and takes her inside the building, on the upper floor. There are several rooms with wooden name plates on door frames: "Paper bags", "Basket weaving", "Crochet & embroidery" and "Play room". Madhur peeks inside each room. The women appear disinterested in their tasks, like they're being forced to do them. In comparison, the farm women seemed thrilled to work. 'Don't they like the work?' Madhur inquires. 'They're on medication,' the sister explains. 'Those outside ones are not—in fact, not all the residents here are mentally challenged. Some are just abandoned by families and husbands.'

Madhur walks to the closed play room. 'Is this for games

and entertainment?' she asks, expecting to see carrom boards, chess boards and table tennis tables.

'No, that's where the severely challenged residents come to do basic co-ordination exercises,' the sister says and opens the door to show her. A volunteer in a bright yellow t-shirt looks up and says hi. She's helping a young girl with close-cropped hair, to place wooden blocks in slots with her un co-ordinated, flailing arms.

Another volunteer is urging an old woman to stack coloured rings on a pole, but the woman sits motionless on her wheelchair. Each time she is handed a ring, she holds it for a few seconds and then slackens her grip, dropping the ring to the floor. The volunteer patiently retrieves the rings rolling in different directions. As one rolls towards her feet, Madhur picks it up and tip-toes to hand it over, not wanting to startle the wheelchair-bound woman. Seeing the old woman's face, Madhur is shocked and quickly leaves the room, running past the sister and continuing till she finds Karl and Jacinta. Seeing her huffing and puffing, Jacinta says, 'Almost done, haan, we'll leave in ten minutes.'

Madhur waits patiently as the papers are signed and attested. Shirodkar Uncle then hands the documents to Sister Mathilda, who is the administrator of the Thivim Home, and shakes her hands. 'It's done,' he announces. 'You all can go now. I'll stay and discuss time frames with Sister.'

As they get up to leave, Jacinta speaks up. 'Karl dear, let's see the place, since we're here.'

'You see it with Madhur. I don't want to. The place looks depressing,' he whispers to her.

'I have already looked round,' says Madhur, before Jacinta can ask her. 'I must be seeing things, but I thought I saw Aunty Coutinho. I got so scared! *Mai bhaag ké aayi!* (I ran away!)'

'Wait!' exclaims Jacinta. 'That must be Angela.' She asks Sister Mathilda, 'Is Angela Coutinho here? Right now?'

'Yes of course,' she replies, 'You can meet her. Ask any sister to take you to her.'

'I'll wait by the car,' Karl tells Jacinta.

'What do you mean by that? She's your cousin! The eldest one in your family. Come, you must meet her.'

'Jacinta, you go, if you want,' he says firmly.

Jacinta takes Madhur's hand and says, 'Show me where you saw her.'

Madhur hesitates, but points to the room upstairs and says, 'There, in the last room. Knock and go inside.' As Jacinta starts climbing up, Madhur decides to join her. They open the door and wait at the threshold. The volunteers gesture that they can step inside. Jacinta sees the old woman and exclaims, 'Oh my god! That's Aunty Mabel from ten years ago!'

The volunteer turns the wheelchair around and tells the old lady, 'Look Angela, your mama's here to meet you,' pointing to Madhur and Jacinta.

Angela follows the volunteer's finger with her eyes and sees them, 'No mamma! No mamma!' she says angrily, hitting the volunteer with the ring in her hand. Madhur and Jacinta look on apologetically as the volunteer patiently pacifies her, whereupon Angela goes limp and sinks into her wheelchair, staring at the wall in front. 'She's been like this since Mrs Coutinho passed away. Mrs Coutinho would visit Angela once a month. Lockdown was the first time in fifty years that she did not visit. And now …'

Madhur starts sobbing quietly, 'She's behaving just like Aunty Coutinho, when she had a stroke.'

Jacinta kneels down in front of Angela, takes her hand in hers and kisses it. She whispers, 'Angela, you'll move to your real home soon.'

CHAPTER 25

Bambai Sé Aaya Mera Dost

In the first week of April, Madhur and Chaitali go on a road trip to Mumbai, to procure hemp fabric, chaperoned by Chaitali's dad, Pradeep Hanjunkar. After a journey of nearly fourteen hours—with a lunch halt at Chiplun—they arrive at Girgaum, late in the evening. They are going to stay at Pradeep's sister, Shreemati Vatsalya Morajkar's house in Fanaswadi for two days.

Older than Pradeep by two decades, Vatsalya was married off at a young age to a Goan in Bombay (now Mumbai), who held a supervisory job in a textile mill in the 1960s. A widow now, Vatsalya's three sons are married and work in corporate offices at Worli and Nariman Point. But she refuses to leave her chawl and live in their chrome and steel residential towers at Nana Chowk. Her Fanaswadi chawl is her world. The sons visit her regularly for chai and chit-chat, and then return to their high rises and their wives.

In 2014, Chaitali had shifted to her aunt's place and to pursue her studies in Mumbai.

'After three years you've come to see me? *Visarli vatt'ta malaa!* (You've forgotten me!)' Vatsalya complains to Chaitali, welcoming them all inside her two room quarters on the ground floor. 'And who is this, *nazuk gori-gori paan* (delicate, fair creature)?' she says, smiling at Madhur.

Chaitali touches her aunt's feet and introduces Madhur, '*Aat'tya, hi maajhi khaas maitreen* (Aunt, this is my special friend), Madhur. She's a famous fashion designer from Delhi, and she is our tenant too.'

'You look as sweet as your name,' Vatsalya says in impeccable English to Madhur. She turns to her brother Pradeep—completely fagged out from the drive, and asks, 'How come you all decided to drop in suddenly—of course, lockdown is over, but people are still being cautious, you know.'

'Ask the girls, I'm just their driver,' he says and shrugs.

'We've come for fabric shopping,' Chaitali says excitedly, 'Madhur and I are taking part in a fashion competition.'

'Arré wah! All the best. I wish your *atoba* was alive, he would have taken you to all the wholesale markets, got you the best rates,' Vatsalya says to Chaitali.

The next morning, they set out to visit a cloth manufacturer in Lower Parel. 'Let's take Raju mama's kaali-peeli—he used to drive me to the college for free sometimes, when he had to pick up his regular customer at Peddar Road,' she tells Madhur. Raju mamma's kaali-peeli is parked at the taxi stand.

'*Arre! Waapas Mumbai?*' (Back in Mumbai?) an old cabbie asks, waving at Chaitali.

'*Sirf do din, Raju Maama. Sab theek?*' (Only two days, Raju Maama. All good?)

'Haan beta.'

Raju Maama takes them via the Chowpatty seaface route, to show them the city sights. Chaitali points out the Mahalaxmi temple, and a little further, the Haji Ali Dargah—which is in the middle of the Arabian sea. 'You must have seen that in the movies—I've walked to it once.'

Madhur looks at the white mausoleum, surrounded by a glistening sea, nary a bridge nor a pathway in sight. 'Walked? How? Like Jesus?'

Chaitali bursts out laughing, 'It's high tide now, so the rocky pathway that leads to it is submerged. You have to plan your visits according to tidal activity.'

'Interesting. Only in Mumbai one has to work hard even to worship God,' Madhur observes. As they go past Mahalakshmi Racecourse, they watch crowds of nattily dressed people exiting big cars, reeking of money.

Chaitali whispers, 'One day, all the high society ladies will wear my outfits to the Derby.'

'No sweetheart, they'll wear mine!' Madhur says confidently. 'No one will wear organic clothes to the races. What if the horses get hungry and eat their dresses?'

Chaitali gives her the side-eye.

'Seriously, you should consider fusion, don't stick to only organic. Bend your philosophy a bit!' Madhur says to her.

They arrive at High Street Phoenix, where the country's best-known hemp manufacturer is located. 'My *Atoba*, Vatsalya *Aat'tya's* late husband, used to work in this mill. Many old buildings have been replaced by malls, five-star hotels and cinema theatres here,' Chaitali says. 'See, they've still kept the chimney though.'

A massive chimney towers above surrounding buildings, emblazoned with the mall logos. At one time, it must have spewed smoke and sweat of the mill worker's toil.

'Looks very cool! Delhi malls are bigger, but they are all glass and steel. This has some character as it's a mix of the old and the new,' Madhur observes.

'Oh yes, you must see some of the restaurants inside, they have high ceilings, wooden floors and big old windows. Yes, it does look interesting,' Chaitali agrees.

'Did I ever tell you that I worked at a mall in Delhi? For two months only, haan…' Madhur says suddenly.

'As a salesgirl?'

'No! I was their in-house visual merchandiser.'

They buy their hemp fabric and do a tour of the mall, stopping for lunch at a gentrified Irani restaurant. Madhur cannot stop praising the quaint restaurant and its food.

'Arré, I'll take you to a real Irani café. Let's go to Kyani's at Dhobitalo,' Chaitali says. 'But we'll go home first and drop these big cloth bundles.'

They return to the chawl by tea-time.

'Madhur, meet my cousins—Shirish dada, Harish dada and Ramesh dada,' Chaitali says, introducing her to three gentlemen who look older than her father. Seeing the look of surprise on Madhur's face, Shirish says, 'I know what you must be thinking! That we look older than her father, Pradeep, no? And we are! Even he calls us "dada", even though he is our mama!' He looks at Pradeep and says, '*Kay re Praddu? Barobar boll'lo na?* (What say you, Praddu, I said it right, no?)'

Vatsalya looks at Madhur and explains, 'This was normal in families before family planning was introduced. We would see our parents having children, at the same time while their grandchildren were also being born. It's unthinkable now, for single children like you and Chaitali, or even my three sons.'

'So, what's the plan, girls? Going out for a party?' Ramesh asks, changing the topic to save the girls.

'We plan to go to Chowpatty first, and then to Parsi Dairy Farm and end the adventure with Kyani's,' Chaitali replies.

'I'll take y'all,' says Harish, he's the youngest of the trio. 'I haven't been to Kyani's since college, I think.'

'No, no, we'll go on our own. It's girl's night out,' Chaitali protests.

'Okay baba! Madhur, how do you get along with her? She's so stubborn.'

'I'm also stubborn. So, I understand,' Madhur says and smiles.

'Goa is so much better,' Madhur muses, as both girls exit their taxi at Chowpatty Beach. '*Patta nahin, log kyon* Mumbai *ké peechein paagal hain?* (I don't know why people yearn to shift to Mumbai?)'

'I love it here! After staying here, I realized that Goa is slow,' confides Chaitali. 'And look at these skyscrapers!'

They walk from Chowpatty to Marine Drive, jostled by the crowd of health freaks, dog walkers and senior citizens ambling along. Some people are wearing masks, but for the rest it appears as if COVID never happened.

'*Yaar, yé itni bheed!* (It's so crowded!) And where's the beach? It's all concrete…'

'Yes, but things get done in Mumbai,' Chaitali argues. 'Nobody tells you to come tomorrow. Did you see how the hemp cloth guy immediately got us the colour we wanted, from their godown?'

'*Waisé toh, mujhé bhi* laptop *ki* battery *immediately dilwa di gayi* (I was able to replace my laptop battery in a short amount of time), in Goa!'

'There's freedom here!' says Chaitali, spreading her arms theatrically.

'Aye hello! Who or what's tying you down in Goa?' Madhur asks.

'Nobody … but over here, people let you be. Goa *mein family ki sunn'ni padti hain!* (I have to adhere to my family's expectations in Goa!)'

'Yeah, I understand that,' says Madhur, 'even I had to leave Delhi, to find my freedom in Goa. Maybe you need to find your freedom away from home—but after the Fashion Week, okay?'

Chaitali stays silent for some time and then she whispers, 'You're right, you know.'

'Oye Chaitali! Don't take me seriously! Why leave Goa when you already have your own boutique there?' she asks.

'You know, after graduation, I had an offer to work at a well-known fashion house here, as a designer. But my baba said, "Come home, why work for someone else?" He built the boutique for me on a section of our field. Had I worked in that fashion house, I would've been a more skilled designer today…'

'Don't worry, we'll put up the best show at the Fashion Week. Then forget Mumbai, you'll get offers to work in New York, Paris, Milan …'

'Mumbai is good enough!' says Chaitali.

'So, tell your family. If they allowed you to study here, I'm sure they'll let you shift here for work too.'

'I could study here only because I stayed with my *aat'tya*. Vatsalya *Aat'tya* is nice, but I want to live on my own, in a rented place. Like you. My parents will never let me do that.'

'Should I speak to your baba?' Madhur asks.

'Arré no! It's my problem, I'll handle it. Your words of encouragement are enough,' Chaitali says and smiles.

The sun sets at Marine Drive, and the streetlights along the 4-km-long curved bay are switched on. 'Look, Queen's necklace!' Chaitali points out to Madhur. 'Wah! Kangana ka?' Madhur jokes. Chaitali looks offended, 'No, British waali Queen ka.'

The raised promenade around the bay is covered with huddled couples, hugging and kissing. 'Now this I like! *Yeh khull'le aam ishk-vishk! Wah!* (All this public display of affection! Wow!)' says Madhur, as Chaitali looks away embarrassed. After spending a great time in Mumbai, the girls return home.

Chaitali and Madhur dive right into work and creating their sample outfits, on their return to Goa. They choose a bohemian look, with an asymmetrical, but fitted silhouette. Hemp fabric is heavier than cotton and linen—it tends to hang heavily on the body. To tackle this issue, they construct the dress in a patchwork pattern of fabric. Cut outs of large hemp leaf motifs—to reveal the wearers' skin—are positioned strategically on the body. For accessorising the outfits, they knit head scarves, shawls and stoles with hemp rope, using a large chain stitch, and interspersing hemp leaf in applique work. Their three sample outfits are in maroon, mustard and olive colours.

The minute their outfits are ready, without taking a break, they start planning their photoshoot. 'Let's go to Morjim and Mandrem beaches and look for Russians,' Madhur says excitedly. 'I think we should hire models with tall and strong body types—not the typical tall and petite frames. A fuller body will showcase our fabric to its full potential.'

Their attempt at hiring Russian models on the spot goes awry sooner than they can say 'Dasvidanya'. Madhur relies on Google Translate, but it's not accurate, leading to some hilarious misunderstandings. The sun-bathing Russians abandon their deck chairs, get irritated and start shouting aggressively at them, "No photo, no photo!" Suddenly, Madhur remembers that there is someone who can help. Going through her phone contacts—grateful that they were restored by Shanx—she finds Ivan Kuznetsov's number.

'Hi Ivan, it's Madhur—"Maddie blogs from Goa", remember me?' she asks.

'Oh Madurai! How's you?'

'Good, good, Ivan. I really need your help. I'm at Morjim Beach and need Russian models for a photoshoot. They don't speak English, and I only know "dasvidanya"!' Madhur explains.

Ivan arrives within ten minutes with Tatiana, his equally tall, designer girlfriend.

'So, you are the famous Madurai!' she says, hugging Madhur. 'Thank you for the logo design. And who is your friend?'

'This is Chaitali, she is also a designer.'

Tatiana happily rounds up all the women they point to. 'I'm curious about your project. How may I help you?' Tatiana asks Madhur. 'You can use some of my accessories, if you want.'

'Thank you! But we can't. The participation guidelines are very strict. The accessories also have to be ours—we cannot use another designer's stuff,' Madhur explains to her.

'I meant smoking accessories,' Tatiana specifies.

'Oh, okay!'

Tatiana does a quick trip to her boutique and returns with rolling papers, vapes, bongs and pipes from her own collection—for the models to use, hold, or be placed somewhere in the picture frame.

They do their photoshoots in locations as diverse as mangrove forests, rocky beaches, riverine estuaries—complete with crocodiles basking on sand bars—and in abandoned, decrepit houses; taking five days to photograph just three dresses.

After the photoshoot, Madhur and Chaitali compile a comprehensive pitch deck for their 'Anjuna' fashion line of organic hemp outfits, and courier it to the Fashion Week organizers.

Now all they have to do is wait for the organizers' nod of approval, and a formal invite to participate in the Fashion Week. If selected, they'll be given three months to get the rest of their line ready.

CHAPTER 26

Runaway Girls

Chaitali shuts her eyes and prays as Madhur tears the top edge of an officious looking envelop—it's from the Fashion Council. She continues closing her eyes, hoping to hear some jubilation from Madhur. After two minutes, Chaitali opens one eye and spies Madhur reading the letter intently, a frown creasing her forehead.

'What?' she asks Madhur, who reads till she reaches the last line of the four-page letter. She folds the letter and hands it to Chaitali, saying, 'Sorry, Chaitu.'

'Kya hua?' Chaitali asks, but Madhur does not respond. She leaves the bed and walks dejectedly to her balcony. As she stares into the wide expanse of flattened, dried brush fields—now being used as football grounds—she can hear Chaitali exclaiming from inside, 'What bullshit yaar!', 'Complete nonsense!', 'Screw them all, man! Bloody bastards!' and finally, 'Aye Maddie! NOW WHAT?' Chaitali steps out into the balcony and puts an arm around Madhur.

'Shit, I feel like smoking. Got a ciggy?' Madhur asks her. Chaitali nods a no.

'Go ask your dad.'

'I'll get from the shop *neeché*, if you absolutely must smoke… but I'd say don't. Not here, Maddie, smoke somewhere else, na?'

'Fine then, let's both go to a bar—far-far away, we'll smoke and get drunk also, chal!'

'I don't know…' Chaitali hesitates.

'What's there to know? Let's take a break! Drink some, smoke some, and then we'll brush ourselves and FIGHT THE FUCK BACK!' Madhur screams. She rushes back inside her room, picks up her wallet, her scooter keys, the envelop, and drags Chaitali by her hand, down the staircase. On the way, they are accosted by Chaitali's baba, 'Where are you two going?' Pradeep asks.

'Just for a ride, Pradeep Uncle. We'll be back soon.'

Pradeep Hanjunkar stares at Madhur as if she has spoken Greek or Latin, and continues blocking their path on the narrow staircase. Madhur finds his behaviour a bit odd. She looks at Chaitali, who looks positively scared.

'*Hum dono Russian models ko select karney jaa rahein hain Morjim. Nangé padé hongé beach pé, bicharé! Hum unko apné kapdé pehenayengé … Aana hain aapko humaré saath?*' (Both of us are going to select Russian models from Morjim. They are most probably lying naked on the beach, so we'll go and give them our clothes to wear. Do you want to join us?)'

Pradeep Hanjunkar immediately moves aside to let them pass. In Konkani, he says to Chaitali, '*Baygin yaat, chodd vell lao naakaa!* (Come back quickly, don't take too much time.)' Chaitali nods.

As they speed away on Madhur's scooter, Chaitali starts laughing hysterically in her pillion seat.

'*Hass mat, seekh lé mujhsé!*' (Don't laugh, be like me!) Madhur says, 'Babe, there's no point in being afraid of parents. Who's the future, us? Or them?'

'Us,' answers Chaitali. 'By the way, where are we going? I'm wearing house clothes. You didn't let me change also.'

'Who cares, *hum influencers thodi na hain*? (Are we influencers?)' she says and they both laugh. 'To Siolim,' Madhur says, punching the air with her fist.

They pass the crowded Siolim market area, and continue on a narrow road running parallel to the Chapora river on their left side, with village houses and shops on their right side. The river is a placid mirror, reflecting the sky, clouds, and rows of coconut palms in between. Madhur rides past the spot where she had shot the video of superstar Ricky Malhotra, and onwards to Oxel, where she finally stops at a small jetty. It is quieter and less crowded here, compared to the Siolim Chapora river side—now crowded with Instagrammers and vloggers, since her viral Ricky Malhotra reel.

It's 5.30 p.m., the sunset is expected at 6.30 according to the weather app on her phone. Madhur leads Chaitali inside Rajesh Bar. It's a small four-table bar, diagonally opposite the jetty. They both sit on the same side of a table, and look outside at the riverfront. Colourful fishing boats are parked just off the road, on a narrow sand bank. In the distance, a ferry makes short trips to and from Chopdem, on the other side of the river.

Madhur orders a beer and two cigarettes. Chaitali asks for a chai. Madhur frowns. 'Look, it's not my habit to force people to drink, *par mujhé pata hain ki* you like to drink, and right now you're not drinking because you think that the old uncle at the bar will go and tell your baba!'

'We don't know anybody in this village,' Chaitali says defiantly.

Madhur laughs, 'Aren't all Goans related?' she asks, taking a drag from her cigarette. Chaitali asks for the cigarette and Madhur refuses, '*Sutta mat mar!* (Don't smoke!) Have a beer instead, or a Coke with Old Monk …'

Chaitali orders a plain Coke, takes a sip directly from the bottle and says, 'My life is over …'

'*Arré kyon?* It's starting now, Chaitu! What you will do now, is what will define you. It's not the end of the road, baby!'

'We got disqualified, Maddie! And I fought with my family—because I was so sure we would get selected for Fashion Week. I feel like an idiot now…'

'You fought? When? About what?' Madhur asks, concern in her voice, correlating Pradeep Uncle's odd behaviour on the staircase with what Chaitali has just said.

'About going to Mumbai. My parents are not letting me go.'

'Wait, what? You're going now only? Chaitu, what if we were selected for FW22? Were you going to dump the collection on my head and run off to Mumbai?'

'No re! My plan was to leave after Fashion Week,' Chaitali says, tearing up, 'But baba said he'll not give me any money.'

'Don't you have your own? You've been running your own boutique for how many years now? Three?'

Chaitali breaks down, sobbing bitterly with deep heaving breaths. Madhur shushes her, embarrassed by her sudden rush of emotions. 'It's okay, we'll figure it out. Just take your money and leave—if you feel so strongly about moving to Mumbai. But it would be better if you go with your parent's blessings. Let me talk to them,' Madhur says.

'Baba is not giving me my money! He says he's keeping it because he spent money on building my boutique, plus he's talking about land rates, and the rent I owe him for three years. I'll have to continue paying him forever. I'm trapped. I can never leave!'

Madhur bristles with anger, 'Are you his daughter or a bonded labourer?' She pacifies Chaitali, 'Okay listen, I don't have much—but I can give you enough for a flight ticket and food for a month. Stay with a class mate—you must have at least one good friend in that city na?'

'Yes, a few.'

'Get a job, and then move to a rental.'

'Okay.'

'Done then, for now just keep a low profile. Continue like normal at home, don't let your parents get suspicious,' Madhur advises Chaitali, 'Your escape has to be planned properly.'

'But I can't go home!' Chaitali resumes crying.

'Arré, why not? Your baba did not say 'GET OUT!' he said 'Baygin yaa' that's 'come quickly', right?' Madhur asks.

'Haan, but he'll ask me if we got selected for Fashion Week, and then I'll have to tell him.'

'Chaitu, did you read the letter carefully?'

'Yes.'

'Till the end?'

Chaitali hesitates, 'My brain stopped functioning after the first para.'

'Haan, I thought so!' Madhur says triumphantly, 'See, when I read it, my first thoughts were also—"Here we go! The big famous designers are screwing with me again." My first reaction was to blame my fate, blame my circumstances, my family background… I thought *ki, agar main rich hoti, toh yeh mere saath nahin hota. Agar main un badey designeron kay saath utth'ti-baith'ti, toh shaayad woh mujhey select kartey.* (If I was rich, this would not have happened to me. If I socialized with the big designers, they would select me.) But, you see, Chaitu, when I read the letter again, I saw that it wasn't so.' Madhur hands the brown envelop to Chaitali. 'Read every line, carefully. Yes, we will not show our Anjuna Line at Fashion Week in Delhi, but … we have other opportunities.'

Chaitali reads it objectively this time. After the first paragraph that states they are rejected, the letter shifts its tone and congratulates them on their imagination, their concept and their presentation. Their clothes are styled, accessorized and cut to international standards. Their pictures look professionally photographed, like Vogue or Harper's Bazaar centrespreads. But, unfortunately, their fashion line glorifies 'Weed Culture' and promotes 'Marijuana smoking'. The Fashion Week is supported by a government body—there is no way the FW22 can showcase the Anjuna Line.

There is even a constructive suggestion by two big designer judges—whose pictures Chaitali has seen, getting baked in Goan night clubs.

"Do not emphasise on the 'Hemp' part, instead, concentrate on organic values, natural dyes, the sturdy fabric—in fact, the stiffness of hemp fabric works great for jackets and suits."

They have been offered entry to Fashion Week if they redesign their line—with a change of name of course. And—if this suggestion hurts their artistic sensibilities—one big designer has offered to buy their collection for his haute couture store in

Hauz Khas. Two personal phone numbers have been provided with times to call.

'So what should we do, Maddie?' Chaitali asks, 'Call them?'

'Of course! Lékin, let's decide first what we want,' Madhur opines. 'And let's ask for a 50 per cent advance, and with that money, you go to Mumbai,' Madhur says to Chaitali, 'But Chaitu, I still don't get why you fought with your parents first only- you should have waited to see if we got selected or not, na? No patience you have!' Madhur scolds her.

'Look,' says Chaitali, 'I have to leave Goa. I didn't want to keep this discussion for later. Since Fashion Week is in Delhi, I thought maybe you might decide to stay back with your mom, or go back to working in Delhi ...'

'I'm never EVER going back to Delhi!' Madhur says vehemently.

'Then come with me to Mumbai! We can live together, work as a team. Madhur and Chaitali. Mad Chai...'

Madhur smiles, 'Wah! Nice name, haan. But babe, Mumbai is your dream. Mine is here, in Goa. Chal, on that note, we should go home, *baygin*!'

'I don't know what to tell baba...' Chaitali says, wringing her hands, afraid to leave the bar. 'I failed again...'

'Just show him the letter!'

Chaitali stares at the sun setting across the river, streaking the sky with orange gashes. 'Baba will scream at me because I failed.'

'Arré yaar! What is this? "I failed! I failed!" *Tera failure say kya ajeeb sa rishta hain, tu please mujhé bataa!* (What is this strange preoccupation with failure? Please tell me?)'

'How to tell you ... my aai-baba think I'm no good. They make fun of my organic fabrics and natural dyes. They say only mad people will wear my clothes—'

Madhur interrupts, 'Wait! *Toh* what's the big deal? My mother does the same—'*Kaun péhenéga téréy kapdéy!*' (who'll wear your clothes!)

Chaitali continues, 'You know Maddie, the only time I ever failed was in third standard. In one subject! Math—but I was allowed to go to fourth, because I had above 95 per cent marks in all other subjects. And yet that eight-year-old girl is what my parents see when they look at me, even today!'

'I feel you!'

'But the problem is, sometimes, even I see myself as that eight-year-old who failed and disappointed her parents,' says Chaitali.

'*Kuch toh kaand hua hoga, téré saath!* (Was there some incident that occurred?) It can't be just about a red line on a report card,' Madhur says, squeezing Chaitali's hand, 'Want to tell me?'

'It's quite silly actually, when I think about it...' Chaitali starts, 'my school used to send final exam results by post—to those students who were on holiday. We had to give a self-addressed, stamped envelope to our class teacher on the last day of exams. Now, in 3rd standard, I knew I had done badly in math. I didn't want to go to school to collect my report, so I gave an envelope and said we were going to Mumbai for vacation. But we were not!'

'*Wah! Shabaash bacchey!*' (Bravo!)

'On results day, my mother was making papads at home—I mean, it's a big occasion. All the village ladies arrive with their *polpat-latni* and roll out papads by the hundreds. There's a community lunch and chai. And it's the children's job to put the papads out to dry.'

'Same thing used to happen in my building society in Kalkaji—when I was in school. Now we all buy ready-made papads.'

'We still make them at home, and even now, everybody remembers that incident,' Chaitali says softly.

'What incident?'

'So my classmate, Kumud, her mother was—and still is, a mean lady. Our mothers used to compete over everything, using us kids as pawns. Kumud's mom told the teacher that I was not on a holiday, that I had lied because I was making papads at home! She actually took the trouble of searching out my envelope kept inside a sack for the Post Office, and then, she opened the sealed envelope to check my marks. She came home with my report card and announced to all the village ladies—and my mother, that Chaitali had failed in math while Kumud had passed in all subjects. I still can't forget the look of disappointment on my mother's face. And the gloating look on Kumud's mother's face. Ever since that day, on any papad-making day, in any house of the village, they still talk about how Chaitali did not go to school to collect her report card because she knew she had failed.'

'So mean yaar! You were only eight! But you know Chaitu, you've done so well since. Don't hold that failure so close, let it go. You cannot change your parents perception of you, but you can change your own, right?'

'This Fashion Week was my ticket out of Shubhangi Niwas, out of Goa,' Chaitali says, tears streaming down her cheeks.

'Babe, you are holding so many tickets in your hands! Why can't you see?' Madhur says to her. 'Just be a little patient. And let's tell your aai-baba that we got selected for FW22. And we'll call the numbers tonight! And from tomorrow, we finish the rest of our Anjuna line!'

CHAPTER 27

Get Out! Into the Spotlight

Madhur's suitcases, her laptop bag, her toiletries, books, camera equipment and her clothes are strewn all over the compound of Shubhangi Niwas, when the two girls return home from their Oxel riverside break, at 8.00 p.m. Both girls are stunned to see the ransacked belongings. They run up the staircase—where they're stopped by Chaitali's dad. Pradeep Hanjunkar pushes Chaitali inside the house, shuts the door, and confronts Madhur. 'Take your things and leave!' he screams. 'You are a bad influence on my daughter. You Delhi people leave Goa and us Goans alone.'

'Okay, Uncleji, I will leave, but it's late now…please can I go first thing tomorrow morning?' Madhur pleads.

'No! Leave now! Go stay with Karl Mascarenhas. I gave you the room because of him—big mistake I made. I'm calling him right now.'

Fifteen minutes later, Karl and Jacinta arrive. Karl parks his car and storms out. Standing near the staircase, he shouts, 'Pradeep, come down!' As Jacinta helps Madhur collect her things, she says to him, 'Find out what happened, don't start fighting right away!'

Pradeep Hanjunkar comes down the staircase. Karl is all set to lunge at him when he sees Shubhangi, Pradeep's wife, stepping down after him. Karl pipes down and says hello to her. 'What's this, Pradeep? Is this any way to treat a tenant? You know there are laws that protect them, no?'

'First ask me what happened,' Pradeep Hanjunkar says, lunging angrily at Karl, as Shubhangi holds him back.

'Tell?'

'That Delhi girl is putting ideas in my daughter's head. Maybe Madhur's parents don't care what she does with her life. But we are decent people. We care for our daughters. We don't send our girls to live alone in big cities and fend for themselves. Chaitali wants to go and live alone in Mumbai, work for a big fashion house there. I told her, "Ok, do it, but live with your *aat'tya*." She said, "No! I want to be like Madhur, I want to live alone".'

'But Pradeep, you sent Chaitali to study in Mumbai. Isn't it natural for her to want to work there? Why blame Madhur for it?'

By now Chaitali has stepped down from her room, she joins them, 'After graduation I had so many offers to work in Mumbai, but Baba didn't let me,' she says.

'How ungrateful you are, I built you a boutique!' Pradeep screams at his daughter.

'Did I ask you?' she screams back. 'You built it so it would be like a cage for me—a golden cage is still a cage,' she says emphatically. 'And I have paid you for the boutique with money earned from my clothes. The land belonged to *Aajja*. You got it for free from him. So why are you charging me for it?'

Neighbours and people on the street have gathered around and are listening intently. Everybody gasps at Chaitali's accusation, followed by hushed silence. Then Karl clears his throat, 'What Pradeep, this is not the way to treat your own daughter.'

'I'm also a tenant for him,' screams Chaitali, 'I'm living temporarily in his house till he can marry me off. Till then I have to pay him for everything!'

Pradeep feels embarrassed seeing the neighbours standing and witnessing their fight. He turns to Chaitali and says, 'I didn't take your money—I don't want it. It's saved in fixed deposits for your future. I asked you to pay me, only because I wanted to stop you from going. But if you want so badly to leave Goa, then go! Go chase your stupid dreams! But when you fail—and I know you will—then, don't come crying back to me.'

Chaitali turns and walks away. She goes and sits in Karl's car with Madhur and Jacinta. Looking out of the window, she calls out to Karl, 'Let's go! I don't want to stay here for even one second.'

Karl looks at Pradeep, and without saying anything, he walks towards his car to drive back home.

When they reach home, Karl storms into the sitting room, throws his car keys and plonks on the sofa. 'Ai Saibaa! I need a drink,' he says to Jacinta, 'Babe, you deal with this. I've had it for today!'

Chaitali and Madhur look guiltily at Karl. 'I'm so sorry,' Madhur says it first. Chaitali starts sobbing. Karl takes his drink and leaves the sitting room. On the way out, he says to Jacinta,

'Make her stop! I've heard too many women crying today—I just cannot!'

Jacinta smiles apologetically at Chaitali. 'Forgive him haan! He's been working hard at his aunt's house—it's become a home for mentally challenged women. Too many issues to fix there, to make it safe for them…'

Madhur perks up, 'What? It's already functioning? So fast?'

'It's 3 months since we signed the agreement. They wanted to send the ladies next day only! But Karl said wait.'

'That's fantastic,' says Madhur. 'You guys are doing such a good thing,' she says to Jacinta.

'Enough about us, what's all this?' What's the reason behind all this drama?'

For the next half hour, both girls take turns to recount their roles in what transpired at Shubhangi Niwas. After all is said, they hand Jacinta the letter from Fashion Week, and wait patiently as she reads all the pages. 'It's 10.00 p.m.,' she says, folding the letter and handing it back, 'you girls are up in fifteen minutes!'

Madhur sets up a conference video call—as directed in the letter—and at exactly 10.15 p.m., she punches the number, propping her phone against a vase on the coffee table. Both girls sit on the sofa's edge in nervous anticipation.

The judges pick up almost simultaneously. Madhur is tongue-tied, so Chaitali says hello. Gathering her wits, Madhur says, 'Good to see you both, after so many years. How are you?'

'Maddie my darling! *Aap batao!* You're looking good! And hi to you too Chaitali!' says one judge.

The second judge cuts in, 'Goa's been treating you well, Madhur Chopdaaa! I luuuuurved your work. Chaitali is a good influence on you, I must say!'

'Chaitali, are you a Goan?'

'Yes sir!' Chaitali says.

'No sir-ing! Call me Rohit, and he's Aditya.'

'So, here's the thing girls ... personally, we are floored by your work, so Aditya here, wants to keep your line at his store. Aditya, you tell them. Let's get the business out of the way first, and then we'll explain why they can't participate at FW22,' says Rohit.

'I luuurved the whole hemp and Goa vibe. The colours, styling, the organic-earth-mother feel—right up my alley! So, I would like to place an order of twenty outfits. I need them in three months. Kinda like the schedule you would've followed if selected for FW22 ...' Aditya says. 'I'll pay you the full amount in advance. Have you girls decided your price-range?'

Madhur and Chaitali look sheepishly at each other, and Madhur says, 'No, not yet ... this is so unexpected. But we can send you a quotation by tomorrow morning.' Looking at Chaitali, she says, 'Actually, this is Chaitali's style. She works with natural fabrics. I just helped her to craft the look, the accessories—' Chaitali interrupts Madhur, 'No, no, sir, she did more than that! We both worked on the line together. Earlier, my outfits used to look like Osho ashram robes, but now with Madhur's touch, they are all haute couture,' she says and smiles as the two men on the mobile screen laugh.

'Hai Bhagwan Rajneesh! But you see, that's the beauty of a partnership,' says Rohit. 'You can't tell where one starts and the other ends ... I'm glad you two found each other. By the way, Maddie, do you still design your resort and lounge wear? You'll make a killing in Goa!' he says.

'No, I don't,' Madhur replies.

'Why darling? You are at the right place!'

'Rohit sir, my initial plans to set up my own boutique in Delhi were foiled by COVID. So, I came to Goa to be a fashion influencer and sell my Madfashions line. I thought I would recover my money, but I've had to sell my outfits at one-tenth their cost. I still have many left... But I'm done with influencing and modelling my own creations,' Madhur says to him.

'Such a shame! But don't give up. This collaboration is great. I also like your pastel colours, soft, sheer fabrics—'

Aditya interrupts, 'Rohit, I need to go, so let's quickly tell them about the disqualification.'

'Yes, so here's the issue. FW is under the aegis of the Ministry of Textiles. Those babus will throw a shit-fit when they see your Anjuna line!' he says and has a whopping belly laugh. 'If it was a private, completely corporate-funded show, there'd be no issue at all,' says Rohit.

'Or if it was any European Fashion Week—as weed is legal in most EU countries. Isn't it funny that the country where it grows abundantly, there's a problem,' says Aditya.

'It's all a political game, let's not get into it. Maddie and Chaitali, share your quotation for twenty outfits. Be reasonable! And let's take this forward. In the meanwhile, keep your passports ready. The minute I learn of a fashion week abroad, I will personally pitch for you guys. All the best! Good night my babes!'

Both girls stare at each other for two minutes after the call, then quite suddenly Chaitali gets up from the sofa, opens the main door of Karl's house, and drags Madhur outside into the night.

As Karl tosses uncomfortably in his bed late in the night, he hears them singing, 'Anjuna, Anjuna, Boom Shaka Laka Anjuna! Anjuna, Anjuna, Boom Shaka Laka Anjuna! Anjuna, Anjuna, Boom Shaka Laka Anjuna!'

CHAPTER 28

Banking on Success

After a quick breakfast, Karl leaves for work. An hour later, Madhur wakes up and shuffles into the dining room. Jacinta is shelling peas at the dining table. 'Want breakfast?' she asks. 'Let's wait for Chaitu to wake up,' Madhur says, and scoops a handful of pods to shell. The two women shell peas in silence. After five minutes, Madhur looks up, with tears in her eyes, 'I have to find a new place to stay. Again! And we have to get our order ready—but how? Chaitu doesn't want to go home, so now we're both homeless.'

'First of all, congratulations!' Jacinta says, getting up and kissing Madhur on her forehead. 'Stop crying! You don't know god's plan,' she says, looking at the altar in the dining room.

Chaitali walks in, rubbing her eyes, 'Who's crying?' she asks. Madhur quickly wipes her face with the back of her hand.

'I'm making omelettes. Have your breakfast first, and then you girls have a lot to discuss. Am I right, Maddie? It's all good, okay?' Jacinta says and pats Madhur's shoulder. Chaitali joins Madhur at the dining table. 'What are you crying for?' she asks.

'I have to find a new place, once again!' Madhur replies.

'Don't worry, I know lots of people who give out rooms, flats and villas for rent. What else?'

'To get started on our twenty outfits, we'll need a workshop or a big room. I'm guessing, Chaitali Boutique is out of bounds for Chaitali?'

'My tailor-master has a big enough room—he and his brother live and work there, it can easily fit two more sewing machines. Both of us can also sit and work there.'

'Chaitu, where will you stay? You also need a place ... or, are you going back home?'

'No! We both can rent a place to stay—for the time being only!' Chaitali adds quickly, before Madhur disagrees, 'We'll finish the Anjuna line, and then I'm off to Mumbai,' Chaitali says resolutely. 'Let's quote our rates for the outfits.'

'Absolutely, let's get some money into our bank accounts, and the rest will follow,' Madhur says feeling hopeful. Seeing Chaitali's expression, she asks, 'Wait, do you have a bank account?'

'No,' mumbles Chaitali.

Madhur pulls Chaitali up to her feet unceremoniously, 'Damn! Let's go to a bank right now. It takes ₹2,000 to open a savings account. You see that bank there,' Madhur points to the street outside the window, to a bank signage in the distance, 'Let's go!'

'Arré! Not there, that's where my baba also goes.'

'There is another bank nearby. Actually, call them, and those buggers will be here before you end your call,' Jacinta says, butting into their conversation, placing two plates of omelette bread on the dining table.

'But I don't have even two rupees with me,' Chaitali says to Madhur.

'Borrow from me, come!' Madhur replies.

Jacinta stops them. 'First, have breakfast. Second, have a bath and change your clothes. And third—give me a minute—I'll be back,' she says and rushes inside.

Madhur and Chaitali sit down to eat the omelette pāo. As they dig in, they realize they hadn't eaten dinner last night. Jacinta comes out and places a cheque of ₹5,000 on the dining table, 'This is my small contribution to your business. You'll have to open a joint account for now—a company account takes longer, and requires company registration number etc,' she says, beaming at them. 'All that will come later.'

'No, no, we cannot take this. Absolutely not! You and Karl have done enough for me, and now for Chaitali,' Madhur says, protesting vehemently.

'Take it! I'm being professional here. Later on, y'all can give me a tiny stake in your company, or discounts on your clothes, or whatever ... I want to be the first to invest in you both, before the bigger guys with the bigger money stand in line outside your door.'

CHAPTER 29

Yesterday, Once More

Chaitali knocks on a tattered wooden door, patched with bits of aluminium roofing sheet and nails. The tailor brothers live in a ramshackle house, with faded yellow walls and oyster shell windows. A pair of identical looking men, around seventy years old, dressed in brown formal suits with thick spectacles framing bug-like eyes, smile at them.

Chaitali cheerfully greets the first twin, '*Ola! Como está, Tio Carlus?* (Hello, how are you, Uncle Carlus?)' Then the second, '*Como está, Tio Pedru?* (How are you, Uncle Pedru?)'

'*Bem, obrigado!* (Fine, thanks!) *Koshem asaam tu*? (How are you) You forgot us only!' both gentlemen speak in sync.

'Tio Pedru, Tio Carlus, this is my amiga, Madhur Chopra. She's a big fashion designer from Delhi.'

'Aaah, hello Ms Madhur. Come in, girls,' Tio Pedru welcomes them inside.

From outside it looks like a large crumbling mansion, but the inside is worse. There is just a tiny, blackened kitchen area with a wooden chulha—probably why the interiors reek of wood smoke and a thick haze hangs in the air. A rolled-up mattress is stacked vertically against a wall. Part of the kitchen has been converted into a work area, with a standing fan and two electric sewing machines. The room is brightly lit with flickering tube lights. There is a large blue velvet sofa, sitting alone in a corner, without any companion chairs. Chaitali walks to the sofa and plonks herself on it immediately, gesturing Madhur to do the same. Chaitali continues talking animatedly with the brothers, switching effortlessly between Portuguese, English and Konkani. Madhur feels vaguely uneasy, she can't quite place a finger on the feeling. Clearly this house had its hey days; the lone velvet sofa, the impeccable suits worn by the brothers—however worn out and faded—tell a tale of a grandeur she can't even imagine. It doesn't seem to affect Chaitali though. Maybe she still sees the lost grandeur. Madhur nudges Chaitali, 'I want to tell you something,' she says. 'Babe, I don't think we can work here.'

'Why? There's so much space!'

'I mean, look around,' she whispers urgently. Seeing the reluctance on Chaitali's face, she says in a much softer tone, 'Okay, don't commit to them as yet. Let's go home and decide,'

Chaitali still looks upset but agrees. They bid goodbye to the old men and step outside. Madhur starts her scooter.

'Kya hua?' Chaitali asks.

'Babe, firstly, I cannot work under tube lights. There's dust and soot everywhere. There are white ant markings all over walls. The floor has no tiles, cement is everywhere.'

'So what? Tio Pedru and Tio Carlus are the best! They come from a long line of tailors—their grandfather used to stitch uniforms for the Portuguese police and military! He had a huge factory … but, now they have fallen on bad days. So, I give them work whenever I can.'

'That's very sweet of you and all, my Mother Teresa! But please look at it as a businessperson. What if your organic clothes get infested with insects and white ants? Did you see how they had kept clothes on the floor, on newspaper sheets? We need an airy workshop with lots of natural lighting and decent fans, if not an AC. I mean, we'll be working twenty-hour-days to finish our order. I cannot imagine spending even two hours inside that house.'

'So, what to do?' Chaitali asks, 'And is it really that dirty?'

'Chaitu, we are making clothes for Fashion Week—okay, for one of its judges. They'll be displayed in a Hauz Khas store. We cannot make them here. Even Bangladeshi sweatshops are cleaner. So, here's what I'm thinking … let's just rent a 1 BHK or two rooms. We eat and sleep in one, and work in the other,' she says to Chaitali. 'Just like the tailor masters, but way cleaner and brighter, with no white tube lights please.'

'Theek hain, I'll check with my friends.'

'Don't be cheap, okay? We have enough to pay the rent for four years, if the rates are reasonable enough!' Madhur reminds her.

Madhur and Chaitali shortlist four places that seem to fit their requirements perfectly, at least on paper. When they meet the landlords and explain the purpose, they are disappointed.

'Sorry, you can't have a tailoring workshop. Our society rules don't allow tenants to run a business.'

'I have an old mother, and your sewing machine sound will disturb her.'

'You both are fashion designers? I'll give you a discount on the rent only if you stitch all my clothes for free.'

Most of their rejections sound like this.

Chaitali wonders aloud, 'Does WFH mean only working on a laptop? We are also working, na?' She throws in the towel by evening. 'Let's storm Chaitali Boutique!' she says. 'What will baba do? Call the cops on me? *Dékhléngéy!* (We'll see!)'

'Arré wait yaar! Let me think ...' says Madhur. Just then she receives a call from Karl. She puts him on speaker.

'Maddie, there's an old rusty Singer machine at Casa Coutinho. It belonged to Aunty Mabel. Do you want it? Otherwise, I'll try to sell it. Must be a collector's item, no?'

'NO! Wait, wait! Don't sell it! I'll keep it,' Madhur says on an impulse. Chaitali rolls her eyes, 'Where? On your head?' she shouts exasperatedly. Karl hears that. 'Chaitu is right you know! By the way, did y'all find a place?' he asks.

'Not yet ... Nobody wants us to get two sewing machines and work in their rooms or even in independent flats. They're calling us a "commercial establishment",' Madhur says.

'Technically, they are right, you know,' Karl remarks, 'Offer to pay more rent,' he advises.

'How much more?' Chaitali screams in the background, 'We are willing to pay ₹25,000 already! This is a daylight robbery,' she says.

Karl laughs, 'Imagine, we Goans do this to tourists day in day out ... Chalo, you girls come here and see the machine.'

'I've already seen it,' Madhur replies.

'Come anyways,' Karl pleads, 'I need to borrow your designer eyes. Help me select furnishings and upholstery. The shop has sent samples, but I can't choose. And I can't depend on the nuns, they have such bad taste—they'll turn Casa Coutinho into a jail, just like the Thivim house.'

'Okay, I'm coming over now,' Madhur says to Karl. Turning to Chaitali she asks, 'Want to come along?'

'Cool. We've accomplished zero today, at least we can choose some upholstery and feel a bit better. Karl, you'll pay us for our services?' Chaitali jokingly asks.

'You'll get wine. Maybe be some sponge cake too. Come, come.'

As she nears Casa Coutinho, Madhur realizes that it's been six months since she left the villa. In the beginning, she missed it every day. Then she got sucked into the excitement of Chaitali's Fashion Week project—she was actually happy for the distraction; it eased the pain in her heart, and helped her forget...

Madhur is delighted to see that the villa has a fresh coat of ice blue exterior paint, with white trimmings. The once wayward garden hedges are uniformly pruned, and the large mango tree in the front garden has a crazy-tile cement embankment at its base—for people to sit and chat. Chaitali has never been here before, she just walks straight into the house. Turning to Madhur—who is engrossed in examining the pebbled path, rose shrubs, money plant on the balcão—she says, '*Ago yo bithar!* (Aye, come inside!)'

'*Yetaam*,' Madhur replies and runs after her.

They enter the sitting room and Madhur gasps. Angela is sitting in her wheelchair, staring fixedly at the portrait of Mrs Coutinho on the sala wall. She turns to look at them, smiles ever so slightly, and points to the portrait, 'Mamma,' she says.

Madhur nods, fighting hard to stop her tears.

'Chal, chal,' Chaitali says to her, '*Pagalon ké pichey mat pad!* (Don't rush to help the crazy ones!)' she drags her inside. 'There he is!'

Karl comes out with a bunch of catalogues. Madhur is now engrossed in looking at the painted walls, the new lights, new shelves—the old furniture is still intact, but there are newer side tables, new rocking chairs, new carpets on the floor—or perhaps the old ones shampooed, she wonders.

'What d'you think? Nice, right?' Karl asks Madhur. She looks around feeling overwhelmed. 'I don't know what to say … 'Bravo Karl!' What a difference! I mean, it used to be so dark, that Coutinho Aunty would keep the lights switched on during day also. It's so bright now,' she says.

'Haha, I just cleaned all the old chandeliers. The show lights on the walls hadn't been cleaned for decades—their upturned bell jars were filled with dead insects! And I replaced all tungsten bulbs with brighter LEDs,' he says, giving the girls a tour. 'See, I had to put grills on all the windows—or the residents can jump out and run away! But I put nice designer ones, not jail type,' he says. Taking them further inside, he shows them the new rooms made by partitioning larger rooms. The ladies inside smile at them. 'Let it be,' Madhur protests, she feels like she's intruding into their private space. 'I'll see later.'

'No problem yaar, they all treat me like their son—I've been here for the last four months, almost daily for six hours,' he says. 'They feed me even. Don't tell Jacinta—but they are such good cooks! I'm getting business ideas!' he says in a hushed voice. Opening one of the new attached toilets—he's built one in every room—Karl shows Madhur the fittings. There are geysers, commodes, showers, hand showers, wash basins, cheerful wall tiles—all spanking new. 'I had to change the entire villa's wiring,' he says, 'and the plumbing—all the old metal pipes had rusted.'

'You've spent a lot…' Madhur says, 'Aunty must be smiling from heaven!'

'Not all of it is me,' Karl replies, 'I had already spent on the hospital and the funeral, so the villagers came forward and donated small, small things. Like, one family paid for all the commodes, another paid for all the new rocking chairs, some people donated their own furniture, like beds and cupboards—all in good condition,' Karl explains to the two girls. 'The Parra parish also gave some money. Then, I asked some of my clients to pitch in … and here we are! It's a community effort.'

'Wow, I missed being a part of this!' Madhur says wistfully.

'I had asked you! Anyway, you were busy with your own work—and why not? I'm so proud of you two. Okay! Now take these,' he says, handing them the catalogues, 'Choose the curtain fabrics—you were wondering why everything is so bright, na? Look, no curtains!'

Madhur and Chaitali sit on a shiny maroon velvet chaise lounge and pour over every page. But Madhur cannot concentrate. 'You got a new chaise lounge made, just like the old one!' she exclaims. 'That's the same old one,' Karl tells her, 'Just got it shampooed, and polished.' She gets up and approaches Karl, who is busy discussing something with a carpenter. 'May I see my old room?' she asks.

'Of course. Nobody will stay there,' Karl says, giving her a key, 'Go see.'

'Why?' Madhur asks. 'Why will nobody stay in it?' she asks.

'Oh! I asked for your room, Stella's room and the master bedroom upstairs to be kept for family use. Uncle Godfrey's big study is now three rooms—all his books have been donated.' Madhur looks alarmed. 'He asked for it, in his will!' Karl explains.

Madhur opens the door to her old room; it is just as she had left it. But the walls have a fresh coat of white paint and the furniture is polished. She walks to her bed and sits on it, lost in thoughts. Chaitali walks inside, looks around the big room and says, 'So this is where you lived before! It is nice, easily three times the size of your room at Shubhangi Niwas.'

Madhur snaps out of her daydreaming, 'I know,' she says and steps out.

'How many women live here?' Chaitali asks Karl, who has come to check on them.

'Twenty, for now, with four nuns. We have space for another four or five. But I don't want to crowd the house, or touch the sitting room ... by the way, did you see Aunty Mabel's mad duplicate?' he asks. 'You're so mean Karl! But I know that all this meanness is for show, inside you have a heart of gold,' Madhur says, looking at him fondly.

'Maybe in another six months or a year, we'll build some more rooms outside, utilize the backyard,' he says.

'What about the coconut grove?' Madhur asks.

'Cut a few, keep a few—enough for the home's use,' he replies. 'They won't need coconuts from 100 trees. I'm thinking of keeping maybe twenty trees and clearing out the rest of the area. They can plant a vegetable garden there. The idea is to be self-sufficient, just like the Thivim House—without the jail-like atmosphere.'

Madhur hesitates a bit and then says, 'Karl ... please don't cut the silk cotton tree.'

'I don't plan to … but why?'

'It reminds me of Delhi,' she says and smiles.

Chaitali tugs at Madhur, 'Come here,' she says and pulls Madhur to a corner. 'Can we have our workshop here? In your old room? It's so big.'

Madhur hesitates, 'I don't know, yaar … It is a good idea, but getting permissions will be tricky.'

'Try and ask him once! We won't have to look further and keep getting rejected,' Chaitali says. 'Ask him right now! Please!'

Karl comes over, 'Ask what? What are your devious minds planning?'

'Oh, nothing,' says Madhur hesitatingly. 'Chaitali here, was just wondering, if we can set up our workshop in my old room? We'll begin work at 9.00 a.m. and work till 6.00 p.m. We won't disturb the residents,' Madhur says in a rush. She pauses and adds, before he can reply, 'It's just a thought! We'll understand if you say 'no'. I'm sure somebody will give us a place where we can stay and work,' she says, looking at Chaitali.

'Yes, you can,' Karl says.

'What?'

'Take the goddamn room!' Karl says smiling, 'Why didn't I think of it before? I mean, it's so appropriate! Aunty Mabel was a seamstress!' He says, laughing with joy. 'And you two deserve to be in this madhouse—y'all qualify!'

The girls start clapping and jumping.

'Girls! Girls! Please don't sing that stupid song! It's stuck in my head—in fact, I'm singing it right now!'

CHAPTER 30

Heyy! Mona …

Madhur gets a call from a high-fashion boutique in Panjim—where she had kept five of her Madfashions outfits at the start of the year. They had applied a whopping 75 per cent mark up over her rate of ₹35,000 per outfit. Madhur had hesitated at first, but the boutique had a clientele that included Goa's elite, as well as celebrities from Mumbai and Delhi. She didn't expect any sales, but was hoping that the exposure would help.

'Our client has bought three of your outfits. Please come and collect your money. And she wants the gowns slightly altered—tighter at the waist. Can you do that on an urgent basis? You can come in the evening at 7.00 p.m. to collect them for alterations.'

'Sure,' Madhur says excitedly.

Madhur arrives at Amalia boutique in Campal, dot on time. She sits in the reception lounge waiting for the client to show up. 'So, have you selected your wedding outfit?' Madhur asks Jennifer, the store manager.

'I'm planning a trip to Thailand in the next few months to do my wedding shopping—it's a lot cheaper than Goa, and their outfits are of good quality,' Jennifer tells her. 'International flights have finally resumed.'

'Don't you get a good discount from the designers at your boutique? There are at least two local designers here, who do western style wedding outfits too,' Madhur says to her.

'No yaa! And even after a 50 per cent discount, without the mark up, I'll not be able to afford it. Also, in Thailand, at one place I'll get everything—table decorations included. It's worth it. Have you been there?' she asks Madhur.

'No, I haven't … by the way, my studio also does wedding dresses and bridesmaids' dresses,' Madhur informs Jennifer. 'We do retro outfits, to revive the traditional hand-stitched embroidery styles. You should come and check it out. Don't go by the outfits I have displayed here—that's my old work,' Madhur says, pointing to two of her outfits still hanging on the racks. 'My style is much better now. And as for table decorations, you can show me what you like and I'll get it done for you. Here's my new card,' Madhur hands Jennifer a visiting card.

'Thanks, I will definitely drop by—oh, it's in Parra! I stay in Mapusa. I can visit on my way to work,' Jennifer says. 'What time do y'all open?'

'At 10.00 a.m. usually, but we'll open it earlier for you.'.'

Jennifer suddenly stands up and says, 'Hello, Mrs Malhotra. How are you?'

Madhur turns to see the client and her heart skips a beat.

Dressed in a lemon green and white polka dotted halter top over fitted white trousers, hair held in place with Gucci sunglasses, Ramona Malhotra sashays in. She smiles warmly at Madhur, extending her hand. Madhur wonders if she should kiss it; the lady definitely looks regal. Regaining her composure, Madhur stands up and shakes hands. 'Finally, we meet.' Ramona says to her.

'Yes, and thank you for buying my outfits.'

'I love them!' she says. Sidling closer to Madhur, she whispers in her ear, 'I want more, but not from here—they have a big mark up, no?'

Madhur is uncomfortable with the lack of space between them. Perhaps it's just her PTSD with the Malhotras. 'Sure, Mrs Malhotra. But first let's alter the ones you've bought.'

Ramona steps out of the changing room in a white organza strappy gown with inky blue shibori tie and die patterns, and a thin piping of bright red satin on its hemline. 'Wow, Mrs Malhotra, you make this outfit look a lot better than I had even imagined,' Madhur says, lifting her jaw back up from the floor. Jennifer stands around beaming from ear to ear.

'So, what do you want altered? It looks perfect to me.'

'I want it tight around my waist,' Ramona Malhotra says, pirouetting in front of a full-length mirror.

'Actually, Mrs Malhotra, that's how it should be. It has to skim your body, fall freely along its contours,' Madhur explains.

'Maybe I can wear a big red belt at the waist then,' Ramona wonders aloud.

Madhur wants to facepalm, but she stops herself. 'Please allow me to style it for you once. See if you like it that way. If not, I'll alter the waist as per your wishes,' she says, and quickly starts scrounging through the accessories section of the boutique. She finds a stole made of red wool, with hanging pom-poms, and drapes it casually over Mrs Malhotra's left shoulder.

'Nice!'

'Want to go ahead with the alteration?'

'No, this is fine.' Turning to Jennifer, Ramona says, 'Please bill and pack this also.' And then, turning to Madhur she says, 'Maddie, wait for me. We have to talk.'

Madhur waits in the reception for Ramona to collect her parcels. Jennifer meanwhile transfers the money to Madhur's account.

As they step out of the boutique, Ramona says, 'Actually, I didn't need any altering. I just wanted to meet you,' she says and smiles at Madhur. 'I'm sorry, our last conversation was not very friendly … please forgive me, Maddie. I spoke quite rudely.'

'I can totally understand. You must have had a tough time with Malhotraji's sudden death,' Madhur says.

They stand near Ramona's white Innova. 'How did you come here, Maddie? Can I drop you?'

'Thanks for the offer, but I have my scooter,' Madhur says, pointing to her brand-new white scooter—the only purchase she made after receiving her share of money from Aditya Sir.

Ramona looks undecided. She puts her shopping bags in the car and says, 'Driver, *gaadi lekein ghar jao, main inke saath scooter pe aati hoon* (go back home, I'll follow with her on the scooter).'

Madhur is taken aback. These Malhotras have a knack for springing surprises and violating boundaries. 'Are you sure? You'll manage sitting pillion? *Aapké baal kharab ho jayéngéy* (Your hairstyle will be destroyed),' Madhur tells her.

'*Fikar mat kar* (Don't worry)—I rode a scooter to college every day,' Ramona says, climbing pillion and putting an arm around Madhur's waist. 'I miss those days dearly.'

'Please can you hold the back of the scooter? I feel uncomfortable with you holding my waist,' Madhur says.

'Okay, baba!' she says, and then, 'Madhur, can we go via Panjim market?'

'Sure.'

In five minutes, they are at Panjim market. Madhur parks her scooter and looks expectantly at Ramona. 'I love this place!' Ramona says. 'I want to buy flowers, and then I'll take you to my favourite coffee place—where I would go during my college trips to Goa. It should be here somewhere—hope it's still around,' Ramona says, gesturing Madhur to follow her inside. Madhur stops for a minute to admire the Mario Miranda wall mural. 'Which college did you go to?'?' she asks Ramona, attempting to make small talk. She cannot understand why the dead superstar's widow is hanging out with her.

'I went to Mithibai College, in Juhu,' Ramona says. 'It's an absolute filmy college—all the star kids and producer's kids, study there. Well, not so much now ...'

'In Mumbai?'

'Obviously!' Ramona says. 'What about you? Where did you study?'

'NIFT Delhi,' Madhur says with pride.

'Wow, it's difficult to get admission there, na?'

'Maybe, I guess. I didn't face much issues with admission though,' Madhur laughs.

'That's because you are so good,' Ramona says. Madhur looks at her suspiciously, but Ramona is engrossed in checking the vegetables and fruits as they weave their way through the late evening crowd. 'There! There! The flower sellers are over there, come quick,' Ramona says, and then holding her hand she pulls her in the direction. They stop at an old lady sitting on the floor, surrounded by pyramids of red roses; she is weaving a thick string, chock-a-block with roses. Like a fat, red-rosed python or boa constrictor. Ramona picks it up—twelve feet in length—and smells it.

'When do you plan to wear my outfits?' Madhur asks Ramona.

'Let's see ... I don't have any functions to attend this week. But that won't stop me! I'll wear it tonight, if you want.'

Madhur is perplexed by her reply.

'Umm ... okay. Do let me know if you need styling for the other two gowns. I could tell you right now...oh, but you left them in your car...,' Madhur says looking deflated.

'So what, come home with me! I'll wear them, and then you can style them too,' Ramona says, winking at her. Seeing the hesitancy in Madhur, she adds, 'Don't overthink it, I'm only calling you for a fitting! *Koi function nahi*! (It's not an event!)'

'Okay then, buy that big red garland string and that one with the white roses,' Madhur instructs Ramona.

'Why?'

'For an idea I have about the styling!'

The old woman wraps the garlands in newspaper and plastic. Madhur keeps the bundles in front, wedged between her feet, as they ride to Parra, to Ramona Malhotra's villa.

Zipping through the lanes of Bokeachi Arradi—a part of Parra that Madhur isn't too familiar with—they arrive at a fortress like property, with twelve-foot-high walls around its perimeter. 'Don't park your scooter outside,' Ramona instructs her as a massive gate automatically slides open. 'Come inside.' Beyond the gates is a vast manicured lawn, with a pebbled path leading to a wooden, Swiss chalet style villa. The surrounding vegetation is all tropical. Four Shih Tzus with satin bows on their head, come running to greet them. They nip at Madhur's legs, while Ramona keeps saying, '*O méré bacche! O méré bacché! Mummy ko kissy do!*'

'Welcome Maddie, this is my home. It's been featured in Vogue and CNN traveller,' Ramona says excitedly.

'Oh, that's nice.'

Ramona leads her to the sitting room, it has an all-white décor, with low furniture, and padded futons all over the floor. Brightly coloured large pillows are thrown here and there by way of decoration. 'What would you like? Beer or wine?' she asks Madhur.

'Nothing, I'm fine, Mrs Malhotra. Let me quickly show you what I had in mind, and then I'll take your leave,' Madhur tells her. 'It's already 9.30 p.m.'

'Babe, you cannot leave without eating dinner. Don't you live nearby? In Parra itself?'

'Haan, but everyone will be waiting for me at home,' Madhur says.

Ramona changes back into the same organza gown, throwing the woollen stole casually over her shoulder, like a dupatta. 'Like this?' she asks Madhur. Madhur unwraps the parcel of flowers and holds the two rose-pythons in her hands, her eyes looking glazed, as if in a trance. Pulling off the woollen stole, she throws it on the floor, and wraps the red rose python six times around Ramona's delicate neck and shoulders. Ramona looks in the mirror and her jaw drops.

'Oh. My. God! Maddie, you're so good! Wow, I look gorgeous,' she says, striking poses and walking as if on a catwalk.

'Take pictures for my Instagram!' she instructs Madhur, handing her an iPhone. Madhur holds it and goes still for a moment.

'Quick, take the photos Maddie!'

Madhur clicks many photos and returns the phone. 'Please tag Madfashions Boutique, my ladies will be happy.'

'Of course, darling. I'll do a partnership post on Instagram,' Ramona says.

'Thanks, now I must go.'

'Hey wait! I forgot to ask you the most important thing!'

Madhur's heart beats a little faster, 'What?'

'I love your work. How can I help and support you?'

'Just buy our clothes. What you're wearing is from my old collection, made in Delhi. You should come and see my new collection, made in Goa and stitched by Goan seamstresses,' Madhur tells Ramona, 'It's far better. I mean, this is good too,' she says and smiles.

'I will definitely come, now that we are friends,' Ramona says and air kisses Madhur.

Just then, a butler arrives with two goblets of red wine on a silver tray.

'You cannot leave without a drink, c'mon! Please? For me. I don't like to drink alone,' Ramona begs Madhur.

'Okay.'

'Frankie, get some kebabs and dips to go with the wine,' Ramona shouts, and Madhur rolls her eyes.

'Wait na!' Ramona says to her, 'you have to eat something with this wine.'

From watching Mrs Coutinho, Madhur knows she has to sniff the wine, look at its colour, swirl it a bit and, after all that performance, take a sip. She does that and raises an eyebrow at the strong taste.

'Nice, na? It's from South Africa!' beams Ramona.

'I wouldn't know any better, just that it is lovely,' Madhur comments.

'Oh, but look at you! You've definitely attended wine tasting sessions, haven't you?'

'My landlady taught me,' Madhur says wistfully. 'When I came to Goa, I only knew to drink beer from cans and have old monk mixed with coke. She taught me how to appreciate feni, wine and gin … but I don't know brands, or grape qualities, etc.'

'How sweet! You know Madhur, I was just like you—simple—but look where life has brought me,' Ramona says wistfully. 'And now, things like South African wines matter …'

Madhur doesn't know where the conversation is heading, so she just smiles.

Ramona continues, 'I am from a simple Gujrati family. My real name is Ramita. But he made me change it to "Ramona". Because he said, Ricky and Ramona will sound sexy.'

'Who?' Madhur asks uninterestedly.

'My bastard dead husband,' Ramona says. Madhur sips her wine silently. 'Oh, I thought you changed your name for films,' she says, after a pause.

'I acted in one film only, with Ricky. And after that, he would not allow any producers or directors to offer me roles.'

'Oh.'

'He treated me like his property. It feels strange when I remember that I was actually interested in his son! Can you believe that?' Ramona looks at Madhur for a response, but Madhur stays silent.

'Sameer Malhotra, his son, was three years my senior at Mithibai. One day, I landed at their bungalow in Juhu for Sameer's birthday party. And guess what? The father started to flirt with me. Ricky Malhotra offered me a role in his film, just like that! I was so thrilled. I mean, isn't that what I wanted? Why I joined Mithibai in the first place? Of course, I said yes. I was on cloud nine. And let me tell you Madhur, Ricky Malhotra was quite a looker fifteen years ago! Better than his son!'

Madhur smiles. 'What about his wife—Sameer's mom?'

'Sapna Malhotra? She had died of cancer.'

'Convenient,' Madhur murmurs.

'I'm certain she got it because of him, that bastard!'

'Oh okay,' says Madhur, hoping to wrap up and leave. But Ramona seems to be on a roll.

'On my first day at the film shoot, he called me to his trailer van and raped me.'

'What?'

Madhur is shocked, hand tightening around the stem of her wine glass and the colour draining from her face.

Ramona is in tears. 'Yes, I was only nineteen. I visited his van thinking that I will rehearse my lines with him. But that bastard …'

Madhur is listening, silently.

'I'm glad he got his just desserts, thanks to COVID. I'm sorry I was rude to you, Madhur, but there was so much pressure from the media. I had to play the role of a dutiful wife devasted by her husband's death. I had to pretend to be angry and sad, while inside, my heart was dancing!'

'I hope you got what you desired,' Madhur says and gets up. 'Mrs Malhotra, it's been a pleasure. Thank you once again and do visit me at Casa Coutinho.'

As Madhur rides back home, she feels strangely light. All this while, she had blamed herself for the Ricky Malhotra assault. In the initial months she spent sleepless nights ruminating over what she should have done differently to avoid it. Should she have dressed more conservatively—not in shorts? Should she have avoided entering his fast car? Perhaps she should have refused his offer of a smoke—yes, she always thought this was the main issue—that men consider women who smoke as having loose morals. In the end, all her soul-searching had led to just one conclusion: she must stop being an influencer. Because of her eagerness to grow her subscriber base, she threw caution to the winds and went along with Ricky Malhotra. As if they could be friends and equals in any world …

How stupid of her to think that influencing had put her in harm's way. Hacker Shanx had correctly assumed that Ricky Malhotra had predated on many more women before her. Madhur feels a tinge of guilt remembering how she had bitten his head off when he suggested an exposé on Ricky Malhotra. She had even balked at his sensible advice of seeking therapy. As she pulls up outside the gates of Casa Coutinho, Madhur has a brainwave.

'Maybe, I should do another podcast with Hacker Shanx— "How to stay safe while being an influencer."

She is ready to talk about it, about what she has learned in hindsight. She takes out her mobile and quickly sends him a message.

CHAPTER 31

Shanky-Panky

SHANX: Hello-hello, I'm Hacker Shanx, and I'm delighted to welcome an old friend back again to my studio. Ola, Madhur! Or shall I say, Maddie? It's great to have you back. Welcome.

MADHUR: Thank you, Shanx! It's my pleasure. Madhur, Maddie, Mad girl—it's all the same.

SHANX: So friends, Maddie came up with the idea of this podcast, and I think the topic we are about to discuss is of utmost importance.'

He stops and fiddles with his Yamaha mixer, playing a background music track.

SHANX: Advertisement alert! Advertisement alert … Slip on your Sennheiser HD 25 Headphones and listen to this podcast. Click on the link below to claim your 15 per cent discount on all Sennheiser audio products, as well as the HD 25.

Madhur smiles wryly, thinking 'What is 15 per cent off on such expensive headphones? I wouldn't buy them even if I got 50 per cent off!'

SHANX: And now, let's get back to Maddie ... So, Maddie, we talked for many days prior about this topic—how to approach it with sensitivity, what points to discuss, what to avoid, and so on, and I just want to say here that I truly appreciate what you are going to do. And, I'm so proud of you. Before I give out any spoilers, Maddie, please begin.

MADHUR: Hello friends, doston, for those who don't know me, I am Maddie and I used to have a YouTube channel called 'Maddie Vlogs from Goa' which is dormant now. I've stopped vlogging, I don't put out content anymore, or do any 'influencing'... and I get asked almost every day—why?

SHANX: Yeaah, Maddie, WHY!!! Why?

Madhur clears her throat and continues.

MADHUR: I want to clarify that I have nothing against influencers or vloggers. I know there are a lot of debates going on right now—is 'influencing' even a real job? And in Goa, there have been reports of a possible ban on them in certain areas ... Even though I don't 'influence' anymore—there is some valuable advice that I can offer. My topic today is 'How to stay safe, while influencing'.

SHANX: Okay, but first, do you agree with all the bad press we are getting? Is that why you quit?

MADHUR: No, I don't agree with all of it, maybe some of it. And I quit because I wasn't feeling safe. I got tired of the abuse.

SHANX: Loaded sentence! Maddie, first tell us what you don't agree with—about the bad press.

MADHUR: I don't agree with the criticism that it is NOT a profession. I mean, look at you. You make a living out of this AND you are making a difference. Also, as this is a new profession, people may have some reservations about it. I mean, there is always a resistance to accept something new and radical. Maybe people like you will pave the way for it and make it acceptable soon!

Shanx pulls his collars up, adjust his 'Hacker Shanx' mask and flexes his biceps.

SHANX: But that's because I'm a Tech Influencer. It IS a real job!

MADHUR: And a fashion influencer's is not? Or a travel vlogger's is not?

Madhur rolls her eyes before continuing.

SHANX: People need to know how to use technology, how to trouble-shoot. In fact, I call myself 'Free Tech Support'.

MADHUR: There is room for all kinds of influencers, Shanx!

SHANX: I agree, Maddie. Now coming to the second issue—the safety measures. But before we proceed, I would like to mention content warning. Serious topics like SA and R-word will be discussed, which may be triggering for some people. So please proceed with caution. Utmost care will be taken while addressing such serious issues, but proceed only if you feel comfortable to do so. As per the regulations, we will not use the full terms.

MADHUR: Thank you, Shanx. So, regarding the safety issue… I admit that I too made many mistakes in my early days, especially when I had just arrived in Goa. I hustled hard for freebies, did all kinds of stunts just to get the right shot, sometimes got into sticky situations, got chased by people and I even got cursed at!

SHANX: Whoa! Give an example, Maddie.

MADHUR: So, there is a photo of me posing in swimwear from my own brand, Madfashions, during my early days in Goa. I went to Ozran beach one morning, when the light was perfect, and sat in the lotus pose on Lord Shiva's head. I got a fantastic shot and the next day I got orders for three swimsuits.

SHANX: Sounds great. So, where's the problem?

MADHUR: Exactly, there was none. And if I had any alert system ringing off in the back of my head, I lowered it down. Please understand that I am not blaming anyone here, but myself. As I was able to succeed and perform such a feat, it boosted my ego and I started believing that I could do anything. You see, I was getting over-confident, and it was blinding me. A month or two later after the swimsuit photo, the Ricki Malhotra reel went viral. And random people started trolling my social media feeds—criticizing old photos, making seedy comments. One extremist group started sending me hate mails, vile DMs and so on. They even started calling me. 'How dare you wear a swimsuit and sit on Shiva's head? You're insulting our culture,' they said.

SHANX: Then?

MADHUR: Then I switched off my mobile, deactivated my accounts and stopped all my activity on social media. Did a full-on detox, and it REALLY helped.

SHANX: Oh, is that why? There were rumours that you gave the old man COVID! I thought you felt responsible for Ricky Malhotra's death.

MADHUR: What nonsense!

SHANX: So, Maddie, that one image brought you under public scrutiny and exposed you to the worst part of being a public figure on social media.

MADHUR: Let me clarify one thing: I'm used to trolling, I know a lot of guys leave double-meaning comments. I mostly ignored them in the past, but this was next level. Mind you, I have been posting videos for a long time, and I was used to mean comments too. But death threats are different, and should not be taken lightly.

SHANX: So, were you like, scared for your life?

MADHUR: I was, Shanx.

SHANX: What advice would you give to new influencers?

MADHUR: Have a thick skin. (*giggling*) And carry pepper spray. Also, put an emergency alarm system on your phone—that contacts five people. Use it if you feel unsafe while shooting outdoors, or even indoors. Keep good relations with your neighbours, your landlord and/ or landlady, if you're a tenant. God forbid, if you get into a bad situation, they will be the first people to help you.

SHANX: Good advice, Maddie, but … (*reaching out to rub Madhur's forearm*) you don't have thick skin, your skin is soft.

Madhur is embarrassed. Shanx kicks himself for making things awkward.

SHANX: Next advise?

MADHUR: In retrospect, I feel I shouldn't have sat on Lord Shiva's head.

SHANX: Really? Why?

MADHUR: I hurt some people's sentiments. Maybe that picture would have looked as good if I had stood beside it. But what I've realized is that as always, women are second-class citizens even in social media. If a guy had done what I did, no one would have batted an eyelid. I mean, I have seen pictures of guys doing obscene things there.

SHANX: Fight the bias, Maddie! Ask for equality! #fightthebias. Let's trend it, friends!

MADHUR: It's not a woman's fight only. Men should also fight the bias. What I mean is, the good men should stop or call out the bad men, the trolls and the haters. Strength in numbers!

SHANX: Agree, agree AND agree! Maddie here's my pledge to you, I'm going to make a bug that will hack into trollers' accounts, infect their mobiles and laptops, then clean out their bank accounts and transfer all the money to the people, personalities, journalists, influencers, actors and activists they are trolling. Howzaat?

MADHUR: (*whispering aggressively*) Idiot! Now they'll know!

SHANX: It's just a threat, Maddie. I can do worse ... but you get my drift, na?

MADHUR: Yes. Sweet!

SHANX: Next advice.

MADHUR: Don't beg for free anything! Pay for it first, and then review it or make videos. Because, in life there's no free lunch,' she says and pauses to breathe. 'If not money, then you'll end up paying with something else. Money is cheaper.

SHANX: Interesting advice, Maddie, but what exactly are you implying? Can you be more specific? Because a lot of us do get free products to review and use.

MADHUR: Only well-established bloggers-vloggers get a lot of offers. Like you, you've been doing it since you were ten—

SHANX: Eight!

MADHUR: Oh yaa, eight ... But so many influencers buy their subscribers and likes, and then they go out and say *ki dekh bhaiyaa, mere itney followers hain* (see, I have so many followers) ...

SHANX: Did you do that?

She doesn't answer.

MADHUR: But I'm happy to see that many young female influencers take their brothers or boyfriends along to hold cameras and reflectors, and sometimes to shoot. That's good! Never go alone, take a girlfriend even, especially if you're visiting unknown, undiscovered places, or meeting creepy restaurant and club owners!'

SHANX: Haha, lets segue into a trending topic right now—#BTS!

MADHUR: 'BTS' as in 'Behind the Scenes'? Or 'Behind the Shoot'?'

SHANX: Nope, as my favourite Aussie blogger calls it 'Boyfriends with Tech Skills'!

MADHUR: Oh damn, I saw his videos too! They're hilarious—but I don't care, take them for support and safety. Because, in India, men will not harass a woman if she's accompanied by another man. *Koi stupid sa code hain tum bhai logon ka.* (It's a stupid bro-code among men.)

SHANX: Not all men.

MADHUR: But of course!

SHANX: Any more advice, Maddie?

MADHUR: In spite of taking all precautions, if you still land in a bad situation, remember that you are not alone. Many others have faced the same or worse situation. Reach out to people close to you. If you feel comfortable, reach out to people online. There are great many websites and helplines, ready to listen to you and help.

SHANX: For our listeners, can you specify 'bad situation'.

MADHUR: A 'bad situation' can be blackmailing, harassment, death threat, SA, R-word or threat of SA and R-word. I cannot specify them all, Shanx. Those who are facing it know what I'm talking about. There are all kinds of situation in life, as well as in social media.

SHANX: So, I want to flex a bit here. After I became friends with Maddie, and she told me about the threats and trolling, I followed the trail of the extremist group, using my hacking wizardry, and guess what we found out?

MADHUR: It was a bunch of teenage guys who lived close to my house, in Delhi. They made a fake account just to harass me. It wasn't any extremist group.

SHANX: Exactly! All trolls are bullies. Fight back and they will back down. And what we did to them, well, that's a secret! Even they don't know. Yet!

> **MADHUR:** (*laughing*) Thank you Shanx!
>
> **SHANX:** Thank YOU, Maddie! And that's all folks! Stay wild, stay fearless! This is Hacker Shanx with Maddie Chopra, of 'Maddie Vlogs from Goa' and 'Madfashions', signing out! See ya soon!
>
> **MADHUR:** Like and Subscribe to this channel, and listen to the podcast on Spotify.

As he walks her out of his house, he asks, 'Wanna go for a drink?'

'Abhi? It's 3.30 in the afternoon!'

'It's 8.00 p.m. somewhere!'

Madhur smiles.

'Maddie,' he says hesitantly, 'I was waiting for you to tell the actual truth about Ricky Malhotra, but yet again you didn't.'

'Like I said before, let it be. *Murdey ko mat ukhaado!* (Don't dig out the corpses!)'

'As you wish, Maddie. But I'm happy to see you are much better now.'

'Haan, Shanx. I'm doing well. I've made my peace with what happened. It wasn't my fault—I've stopped blaming and shaming myself. As recently as a week ago, I think I had a breakthrough.'

'That's great.'

'Shanx, so many things are going great for me, so I focus on those things. So many people have been good to me—my god, I'm blessed! There was Coutinho Aunty—May God rest her soul—there's Karl and Jacinta, Chaitali, the nuns and the women at Casa Coutinho. And you.'

'Me?'

'Yes, you!' she says shyly.

Shankar Sardessai can't wipe the grin off his face. 'So, Arbor?'

'*Arré, koi aur jagaa dhoond na!* (Suggest a better place!) All the time Arbor, Arbor!'

CHAPTER 32

Fashionably Mad

Madhur wakes up to the constant ring of her phone, and rushes to answer the call. It's 3 a.m., and she's pretty sure it's Chaitali calling from Delhi, without looking at the phone. Chaitali is attending the Fashion Week as a VIP guest, on a special invite from Aditya and Rohit. Madhur had also received the invite, but she chose to not attend.

'Chaitu! It's so late!'

'I know, I know, but I had to call!' Chaitali speaks excitedly over the din of loud background music.

'*Kya hua?*' Madhur asks, as she walks back to bed and flops on it, her phone glued to her ears. Suddenly, she gets a video call request from Chaitali. The girl's gone bonkers, Madhur thinks while swiping to accept it. Chaitali appears on her screen, dressed in a blue sequinned Madfashions top, and it looks like she's at a discotheque.

'I'm at an after party in a Delhi farmhouse! Can you believe it? It's so crazy here! I barely know anybody—and guess what? I'm fine!' she says.

'*Jeeyo mere lall!* (Live long, my child!)' says Madhur. '*Mojheam navaar gin maar don-chaar!* (Have a few gins for me!)' she says in Konkani.

'Ché-ché! No gin-bin!' Chaitali replies, '*Bahut kuch peeliya!* (Had a lot to drink!) Also, DJ bhaiya is my schoolfriend from Goa!'

'At least you know one person there—the most important one! Okay, let me sleep now,' says Madhur. 'I have work tomorrow.'

'Madhur, wait, I met your mom!' Chaitali shouts excitedly.

'What? How—I mean where?'

'She visited the Fashion Week venue and was asking about you. Incidentally, Aditya Sir overheard her and called me immediately to meet her.'

'Oh ... I haven't called her this entire month,' Madhur says guiltily.

'Bitch! Anyway, your mom was asking me about you. Have you told her about Madfashions?'

'No ...'

'Why yaar? She is worried about you. You know, from your description, I always imagined her to be, like, horrible! But she is so cute and sweet, Maddie! She's shorter than you!'

'She's sweet to you, darling, to you!'

'Anyway, your mummyji has asked me to convey a message to you. She said that you should stay in Goa only, if you like it so much. She said something about the biraadri not liking you, they may create trouble ... I didn't understand that part very well. Please call her, and she'll tell you.'

'Ya, ya, she always threatens me with that. The biradri can honour kill my arse!' Madhur says and chuckles.

'What the fuck! No shit! Really?'

'Yes, shit! But who cares? *Chal, ab bas kar!* I am falling asleep,' she says while suppressing a yawn.

'Wait! Before you go, there is one more thing I need to tell you! I got a job, Maddie!' shouts Chaitali.

'Bitch, where? *Tu Dilli mein kaam karegi?* (You'll work in Delhi now?)'

'Yes!'

'Chaitali, are you're okay? Or have you had too much Boom Shaka Laka? Be careful of these Delhi farmhouse parties, babe. They do some nasty stuff there.'

'No nasties! And I can take care of myself, Maddie! But hear me out! Aditya Sir has offered me a job as a designer! By the way, our collection is displayed so well at Aditya Sir's store. And they already sold twelve outfits!' Chaitali says breathlessly.

'Oh my God! That's great news. But are you sure about Delhi? *Tera sapna toh* Mumbai *tha!* (Your dream was to shift to Mumbai!)'

'I know, but I'm finally able to leave Goa, no? That's all that matters! And besides, it's okay to adjust your dreams a bit, no?'

'Wow, congratulations, Chaitu!'

'Also, Aditya Sir is open to having us as a team. Come join me? We'll work together!'

'No, darling! I'm not interested in his offer. At one time I would have been ... but you see, *maine bhi apna* dream *thoda adjust kar diya* (I have adjusted my dream too)! I'll explain when you come back. Chal, goodnight! *Phirse jagaana mat!* (Don't wake me again!)'

Next morning, there's a spring in Madhur Chopra's steps, as she does the rounds of her workshop. A row of five modern

Singer sewing machines are being operated by five young ladies. A second row of five old style Singer, Usha and Merrit sewing machines are being operated by five old women. Madhur walks in the aisle and goes to the machine kept at the head of the room, facing the ladies. It is Mrs Coutinho's Singer machine, which belongs to Madhur now.

When she started the workshop, some of the older ladies already knew how to operate the old sewing machines—which were donated by the people of the village. The younger ladies had to be trained to operate the modern ones—which were donated by Karl and Jacinta. Madhur, along with Chaitali's tailor masters, took a month to train them.

Madhur herself took two weeks to learn Mrs Coutinho's Singer. It wasn't easy using the foot pedal. Initially, she'd press it down counter-clockwise instead of clockwise! And she was just amazed to see how the needle speed depended on her pedalling speed. She learnt how to get the most intricate work done by regulating her pedalling. With these old machines, she actually felt like she was the master, not the other way around.

Madhur opens the wooden cabinet and loads her thread bobbin. On cue, the door opens and a young nun wheels Angela inside. Madhur gets up and helps the nun lift Angela out of her wheelchair. They place her on the floor beside Madhur's sewing machine, and Angela immediately crawls underneath the platform and starts playing with fabric pieces fallen on the floor. This is her daily routine.

Angela loves listening to the rhythmic sound of the machine's pedal. It calms her, like nothing else in the world. She associates sounds with memories, and the sound of a sewing machine is connected with the memory of her mother. Of the times when Mrs Coutinho would visit the orphanage and spend the entire day stitching clothes, hemming curtains, and repairing torn bedsheets.

The first time Angela heard Madhur operating her sewing machine, she said, 'Mamma! Mamma is here!' to everybody's surprise. She begged to be taken to the machine. And then she crawled down and lay under its platform.

'Maybe she recognizes the sound of her mother's machine,' Karl explained to Madhur. 'And thinks you are her mother?'

'But Mrs Coutinho only used the Thivim House sewing machines, not her personal one, when she went to visit. How could Angela have heard this particular machine before?' Madhur wondered aloud.

Jacinta smiled and said, 'You know Maddie, they say that some people can remember sounds from the time they were in their mother's womb. Especially, special people like Angela.'

Madhur looks at her phone—it's 7.00 p.m. already. How quickly the day has passed. Angela is asleep at her feet. Sister Lalita, two other ladies and Madhur carry Angela to her room and tuck her in her bed. There's a portrait of Mrs Coutinho in Angela's room, it is a copy of the official one in the sitting room. 'You go get ready,' Sister Lalita tells Madhur.

Madhur rushes to her own room, opens her wardrobe and quickly slips into a pale yellow satin sheath dress. She admires the delicate embroidery on the hem, done by one of the ladies. As she's combing her hair, she hears the distinctive sound of his bike at a distance. Madhur runs outside to stop him before the noise disturbs everyone in the villa. He does as told and starts walking towards Casa Coutinho. On her way out of the compound, Madhur switches on the neon signage of the house boutique, built as an annexe to Casa Coutinho, in the same architectural style.

As she takes her new scooter out of the garage, Madhur smiles at the neon signage reflecting in her rear-view mirror. She feels proud of the work which goes on there.

'*Baygin yo marrey! Kitlo sloooow cholta!* (Come quickly man! How slowly you walk!)' she says, as he approaches her.

Shankar Sardessai sits pillion—in an uncomfortable position—but who'll argue with Mad Chopra?

The End

Acknowledgements

I have spent two decades in my ancestral village of Parra in north Goa, close to the *Dear Zindagi* road, and I have witnessed the assault on what used to be my walking/jogging path, and a regular thoroughfare for locals too. So, in effect, this story was born out of anger, and I hope it ended in understanding.

I wrote feverishly, in a short burst of two months, in between several design projects that had dragged or stalled, frustrating me. I thought that writing was a better way of processing my anger, than going outside and punching an influencer.

I want to thank my agent, Anish Chandy, for believing in my manuscript. Likewise, the editors at HarperCollins—Poulomi Chatterjee, Rashmi Menon and Shreya Mukherjee—for their valuable feedback. A big thank you to Aashim Raj for the lovely cover design, and apologies for all the nitpicking!

I follow many influencers, who do conscious and responsible influencing. I suspected that they didn't even set out to be influencers, and they were just documenting and recording their passions. Later, when I spoke to some (and some are friends) my suspicions were confirmed.

ACKNOWLEDGEMENTS

I want to thank Clarice Vaz (@claricevaz318) for her work in documenting Goa's heritage and traditions, via her lively and artistic social media feeds. Jade D'sa (@thatgoangirl) for her delightful travel and food blogposts. I'm not a foodie, so I consume Jade's posts in lieu of food. Nicole Suares (@tlc_missnic_goa), founder of Content Life Media, for her photojournalism and social commentary. I am drawn to Nicole's feed by the strength of her photography.

My gorgeous friend Mubina Ansari, for pestering me to click so many pictures of her in Goa. Photographing Mubina gave me an insight into what an influencer looks for in a picture, how they curate their feed and what they like to project.

I'm grateful to Ben Antao of GoaWriters for reading my manuscript patiently, giving me valuable feedback and pushing me to 'show more, tell less'.

To Viktoria Fernandes, for vetting the Russian dialogue.

To Heta Pandit, for the mention of her house Maia in Saligão, with its lovely mural of Sacrula, painted by Solomon Souza (grandson of F.N. Souza).

To Arbor in Saligão and Vision Hospital in Mapusa—I've spent time at both places and only have good things to say. (However, Arbor is not exactly opposite Heta's house, it's a little further.)

To my community of writers—GoaWriters, who inspire me and push me to write better.

In gratitude to Keith Fernandes and Jackie Lobo Fernandes for being my Karl and Jacinta, and helping me in my early days in Goa, when graphic design was considered useless (clients didn't want to pay for design, because printers did it for free) and perhaps, graphic designers were as hated then, as influencers are today.

But there's hope. I pray that the tide turns, and we appreciate the value that influencers bring to our lives. I pray for more professionalism on their part, as they help in the growth of the profession, while they grow up and evolve too.

About the Author

Bina Nayak is an author and graphic designer based out of Goa. She was head of Walt Disney's design team in India. Her first novel, *Starfish Pickle: A Goan Adventure*, has been adapted into a major motion picture. After graduating from Sir JJ School of Art she worked in FCB Speer, DDB Mudra, Leo Burnett and Ogilvy.

HarperCollins *Publishers* India

At HarperCollins India, we believe in telling the best stories and finding the widest readership for our books in every format possible. We started publishing in 1992; a great deal has changed since then, but what has remained constant is the passion with which our authors write their books, the love with which readers receive them, and the sheer joy and excitement that we as publishers feel in being a part of the publishing process.

Over the years, we've had the pleasure of publishing some of the finest writing from the subcontinent and around the world, including several award-winning titles and some of the biggest bestsellers in India's publishing history. But nothing has meant more to us than the fact that millions of people have read the books we published, and that somewhere, a book of ours might have made a difference.

As we look to the future, we go back to that one word— a word which has been a driving force for us all these years.

Read.

Harper Collins

4th

HARPER PERENNIAL

HARPER BUSINESS

HARPER BLACK

हार्पर हिन्दी

HarperCollins *Children'sBooks*

HARPER DESIGN

HARPER VANTAGE

Harper Sport